Praise for *The List of My Desires*

'*The List of My Desires* asks what happens when we achieve our heart's desire, after its protagonist Jocelyne wins the EuroMillions lottery'

Harper's Bazaar

'Impeccably translated from French by Anthea Bell, it's a sparkling and intriguing read . . . This is a very elegant novel. Its restraint is wonderful, with not a superfluous word. Grégoire Delacourt's keen eye pans deftly across the inner landscape of desire and longing, presenting a tender homage to almost unfashionable virtues – loyalty, duty, patience – without ever taking the high moral ground . . . These days, it is regarded as clichéd and hyperbolic to describe a novel as a tour de force. But I can't think of a more appropriate description for this book'

Irish Independent

'[A] charming, cautionary French tale'   *The Lady*

'In a short, bittersweet novel, the desires of the heart and the dilemmas of living are braided together with such tender humour and natural pathos that we become as bereft and beguiled as Jo herself'

Saga magazine

'*The List of My Desires* has a natural charm and a clear sense of accomplishment' *L'Express*

'A sweet and poignant novella and its existential themes are redolent of that other French classic, *The Little Prince*. Beautifully written, readers will devour it in one sitting, turning the final page with one adage in their heads: the other man's grass is not always greener' *Irish Examiner*

'An affecting story of a couple thrown into turmoil by their dreams and longings. A beautiful tale' *Psychologies*

'This charmingly Gallic look at how we evaluate our life and the potentially corrosive effects of money is reminiscent of *The Elegance of the Hedgehog*' *Bookseller*

'This thought-provoking debut from Grégoire Delacourt is a huge bestseller in France' *Good Housekeeping*

'This moving novel about the search for happiness has already sold more than half a million copies in France. It's the story of 47-year-old Jocelyne, a haberdashery-shop owner who lives in a provincial

French town with her husband and two children. Her life is enjoyably simple until she wins 18 million euros on the lottery . . . This heart-breaking book is brilliantly written'   marieclaire.co.uk

'*The List of My Desires* is a gorgeous little novel . . . a fable-like tale of how money can't buy happiness'
                                                        Stylist

'A runaway bestseller that looks set to follow the success of *The Elegance of the Hedgehog*. But that's not surprising – Grégoire Delacourt is an author who knows how to make his readers feel happy . . . [he] describes the dilemmas of the heart and the vagaries of fate with tenderness and empathy'   *Elle*

'A massive seller across Europe, this little book of Gallic charm is likely to warm British hearts too'
                                                        Choice

Grégoire Delacourt was born in Valenciennes in 1960. His first novel, *L'Écrivain de la Famille*, was published in 2011 and won five literary prizes, including the Prix Marcel Pagnol and the Prix Rive Gauche. *The List of My Desires* has been a runaway number-one bestseller in France, with rights sold in twenty-seven countries. *On ne voyait que le bonheur*, available from W&N as *We Only Saw Happiness*, was longlisted for the Prix Goncourt in 2014. Grégoire lives in Paris, where he runs an advertising agency with his wife.

Also by Grégoire Delacourt

The First Thing You See
We Only Saw Happiness

the list

of my

desires

Grégoire Delacourt

Translated from the
French by Anthea Bell

A W&N PAPERBACK

First published in Great Britain in 2013
by Weidenfeld & Nicolson
This paperback edition published in 2014
by Weidenfeld & Nicolson,
An imprint of the Orion Publishing Group Ltd
Carmelite House, 50 Victoria Embankment
London EC4Y ODZ

An Hachette UK Company

13

A CIP catalogue record for this book
is available from the British Library

ISBN 978-1-780-22425-1

This book is supported by the Institut français (Royaume-Uni) as
part of the Burgess programme (www.frenchbooknews.com)

ROYAUME-UNI

Printed and bound by CPI Group (UK) Ltd, Croydon, CR0 4YY

www.orionbooks.co.uk

For the girl sitting on the car;
yes, she was there.

Sorrow is allowed, sorrow is advised;
all we have to do is let go, all we have
to do is love.

Le Futur intérieur, Françoise Leroy

We're always telling ourselves lies.

For instance, I know I'm not pretty. I don't have blue eyes, the kind in which men gaze at their own reflection, eyes in which they want to drown so that I'll dive in to rescue them. I don't have the figure of a model, I'm more the cuddly sort – well . . . plump. The sort who takes up a seat and a half. A man of medium height won't be able to get his arms all the way round me. I don't move with the grace of a woman to whom men whisper sweet nothings, punctuated by sighs . . . no, not me. I get brief, forthright comments. The bare bones of desire, nothing to embellish them, no comfortable padding.

I know all that.

All the same, when Jo isn't home I sometimes go up to our bedroom and stand in front of the long mirror in our wardrobe – I must remind Jo to fix it to the wall before it squashes me flat one of these days while I'm in the midst of my *contemplation*.

Then I close my eyes and I undress, gently, the way no one has ever undressed me. I always feel a little cold; I shiver. When I'm entirely naked, I wait a little while before opening my eyes. I enjoy that moment. My mind wanders. I dream. I imagine the beautiful paintings of languid bodies in the art books that used to lie around my parents' house, and later I think of the more graphic bodies you see pictured in magazines.

Then I gently open my eyes, as if lifting the lids in slow motion.

I look at my body, my black eyes, my small breasts, my plump spare tyre, my forest of black hair, I think I look beautiful, and I swear that, in that moment, I really *am* beautiful, very beautiful even.

My beauty makes me profoundly happy. Tremendously strong.

It makes me forget unpleasant things. The haberdashery shop, which is quite boring.

The chit-chat of Danièle and Françoise, the twins who run the Coiff'Esthétique hair salon next door to my shop, and their obsession with playing the lottery. My beauty makes me forget the things that always stay the same. Like an uneventful life. Like this dreary town, no airport, a grey place – there's no escape from it and no one ever comes here, no heart-throb, no white knight on his white horse.

Arras. Population 42,000, 4 hypermarkets, 11 supermarkets, 4 fast-food outlets, a few medieval streets, a plaque in the Rue du Miroir-de-Venise telling passers-by and anyone who may have forgotten that Eugène-François Vidocq,

3

an early private eye, was born here on 24 July 1775. And then there's my haberdashery shop.

Naked and beautiful in front of the mirror, I feel as if I'd only have to beat my arms in the air and I could fly away, light and graceful. As if my body might join the bodies in the art books lying about my childhood home. And then it would be as beautiful as them. Definitely.

But I never dare try.

The sound of Jo downstairs always takes me by surprise. It tears the silk of my dream. I get dressed again double quick. Shadows cover the clarity of my skin. I know about the wonderful beauty beneath my clothes, but Jo never sees it.

He did once tell me I was beautiful. That was over twenty years ago, when I was little more than twenty. I was wearing a pretty blue dress with a gilt belt, a fake touch of Dior about it; he wanted to sleep with me. He complimented me on my nice clothes.

So you see, we always tell ourselves lies.

Because love would never stand up to the truth.

Jo is Jocelyn. My husband for the last twenty-one years.

He looks like Venantino Venantini, the handsome actor who played Mickey with the stammer in *The Sucker* and Pascal the hitman in *Crooks in Clover*. A firm jaw, piercing eyes, an Italian accent that would have you fainting with pleasure, suntanned skin, dulcet tones that would give a girl goosebumps, except that my own Jocelyno Jocelyni weighs ten kilos more than the film star and has an accent that's a long way from turning a girl's head.

He's been working for Häagen-Dazs since they opened their factory here in 1990. He earns two thousand four hundred euros a month. He dreams of a flat-screen TV instead of our old Radiola set. And a Porsche Cayenne. And a nice fireplace in the living room. A complete set of James Bond films on DVD. A Seiko watch. And a younger, prettier wife, but he doesn't tell me that bit.

We have two children. Well, three, in fact. A boy, a girl and a corpse.

Romain was conceived on the evening when Jo told me I was beautiful, and on account of that lie I lost my head, my clothes and my virginity. There was one chance in thousands that I'd fall pregnant the very first time, and it happened to me. Nadine arrived two years later, and after that I never returned to my ideal weight. I stayed large, a sort of empty pregnant woman, a balloon full of nothing.

An air bubble.

Jo stopped thinking I was beautiful, he

stopped touching me. He hung out in front of the Radiola in the evenings, while eating the ice cream they gave him at the factory and drinking Export 33 beers. And I got into the habit of falling asleep on my own.

One night he woke me. He had a hard-on. He was drunk, and he was crying. So I took him inside me, and that night Nadège made her way into my belly and drowned in my flesh and my sorrow. When she came out eight months later she was blue. Her heart was silent. But she had beautiful fingernails and long, long eyelashes, and although I never saw the colour of her eyes, I'm sure she was pretty.

On the day of Nadège's birth, which was also the day of her death, Jo laid off the beers. He broke things in our kitchen. He shouted. He said life was lousy, life was shit, fucking shit. He hit his chest, his forehead, his heart, the walls. He said life was too short. It wasn't fair. You want to rescue what you can from all the shit because time is not on your side. My baby, he added, meaning Nadège, my little girl, where are you? Where are you, poppet? Romain and Nadine were scared and went to their room, and that evening Jo began dreaming of the nice things that would make life sweeter and blunt the pain. A flat-screen TV. A Porsche Cayenne. James Bond. And a pretty woman. He was sad.

My parents called me Jocelyne. There was one chance in millions that I'd marry a Jocelyn, and that one chance came my way. Jocelyn and Jocelyne. Martin and Martine. Louis and Louise. Laurent and Laurence. Raphaël and Raphaëlle. Paul and Paule. Michel, Michèle. One chance in millions.

And it happened to me.

I took over the haberdashery shop the year I married Jo.

I'd already been working there for two years when the owner swallowed a button as she was biting it to make sure it was genuine ivory. The button went down the wrong way, it slipped over her moist tongue, got into her laryngopharynx, hit a cricothyroid ligament and stuck in her trachea, so Madame Pillard didn't hear herself choking to death, and I didn't hear her either, because the button stifled any sound.

It was the noise of her fall that alerted me.

As her body collapsed, it brought down the button boxes with it, eight thousand buttons rolling round the little shop, and the first thing that occurred to me when I saw the scene of devastation was: how many days and nights would I be spending down on all fours, sorting out those eight thousand buttons? Fancy buttons, metal buttons, wooden buttons, buttons for children's clothes, fashionable buttons.

Madame Pillard's adopted son came from Marseille for the funeral, suggested I might like to take over the shop, the bank agreed and on 12 March 1990 an artistic sign painter came to inscribe the words *Jo's Haberdashery, formerly Maison Pillard* above the display window and on the door of the little shop. Jo was proud. *Jo's Haberdashery*, he said, puffing himself up like a man whose chest is covered with medals, I'm Jo, that's my name!

I looked at him, and I thought how handsome he was, and I decided I was lucky to have him for a husband.

That first year of our marriage was brilliant. The haberdashery shop. Jo's new job at the factory. And waiting for the birth of Romain.

But so far the haberdashery shop has not done very well. I have to compete with 4 hypermarkets, 11 supermarkets, the sinfully low prices of the dressmaking stall at the Saturday market, the economic crisis making people scared and mean and the laziness of the ladies of Arras, who prefer the ease of ready-to-wear to the creativity of making your own clothes.

In September, customers come to order nametapes to be sewn or ironed on to school uniforms, and they buy a few zip fasteners and needles and thread when they want to mend last year's clothes instead of buying new ones.

Christmas is fancy-dress time. The princess costume remains top of the pops, followed by the strawberry and pumpkin costumes. For boys, pirates are a good bet, and last year saw a craze for sumo wrestlers.

Then everything calms down until spring. I sell a few workboxes, two or three sewing machines and fabric by the metre. While I wait for a miracle, I knit. The items I knit sell quite well, especially the blankets for newborn babies, and the scarves and pullovers made of cotton crochet thread.

I close the shop between twelve and two and go home to have lunch on my own. Or sometimes, if it's fine, Danièle and Françoise and I have a sandwich at a table outside L'Estaminet or Café Leffe on the Place des Héros.

The twins are pretty. Of course I know they exploit me to set off their small waists, long legs and clear, doe-like, deliciously startled eyes. They smile at men lunching on their own or with their partners, they simper, they sometimes coo. Their bodies cast out messages, their sighs are bottles thrown into the sea, and sometimes a man picks up one of those bottles and there's just time for a cup of coffee, a whispered promise, disillusionment – men have so little imagination. After that, we go back to reopen our shops. It's always then, on the way back, that our lies rise to the surface once more. I'm sick and tired of this town, I feel like I'm living inside a tourist leaflet, oh, I'm suffocating! says Danièle. This time next year I'll be far away in the sun, I'll have a breast job. If I had money, adds Françoise, I'd give up all this overnight, just like that.

What would you do, Jo?

I'd be beautiful and slender and no one would lie to me, I wouldn't even lie to myself. But I don't say anything, I simply smile at the pretty twins. I simply lie.

When none of us has any customers, they're always offering me a manicure or a blow-dry or a facial or a nice chat, as they call it. Meanwhile I knit them berets and gloves that they never wear. Thanks to them, I may be plump but I'm also well groomed and manicured; I'm up to date with who's sleeping with whom, the problems Denise from the Maison du Tablier is having with her consumption of that treacherous substance Loos gin, 49° proof, and the various problems of the girl who does the retouching at Charlet-Fournie and who has put on twenty kilos since her husband fell for the shampoo girl at Chez Jean-Jac, and all three of us have the impression that we are the most important people in the world.

Well, in Arras.

In our street, anyway.

So there it is. I'm forty-seven years old.

Our children have left home. Romain is in Grenoble, in his second year on a business studies course. Nadine is in England, babysitting for people and making camcorder films. One of her films was screened at a festival where she won a prize, and after that we lost her.

The last time we saw her was at Christmas.

When her father asked what she was doing, she took a little camera out of her bag and connected it up to the Radiola TV set. Nadine doesn't like words. She's said very little ever since she learnt to talk. She never said: Maman, I feel hungry, for instance. She just got up and helped herself to something to eat. She never said: Get me to recite my poem, my lesson, my multiplication tables. She kept words safe inside her, as if they were a rare commodity. We conjugated silence, she and I: glances, gestures, sighs instead of subjects, verbs, complements.

Black and white pictures came up on the screen: trains, railway tracks, points. At first it was all very slow, then it gradually speeded up, images were superimposed on each other, the rhythm of it all was spellbinding, fascinating; Jo got up to fetch a non-alcoholic beer from the fridge, but I couldn't take my eyes off the screen. I took my daughter's hand, *subject*, waves went through my body, *verb*, Nadine smiled, *complement*. Jo was yawning. I was crying.

When the film was over Jo said: In colour on a flat screen and with sound, your film wouldn't be at all bad, my girl, and I said, Thank you, Nadine, thank you, I don't know what you were saying in your film but I *really* did feel some-thing. She disconnected the little camera from the Radiola and whispered, looking at me: I was writing Ravel's *Bolero* in pictures, Maman, so that deaf people could hear it.

Then I hugged my daughter, I hugged her to my flabby flesh and I let my tears flow, because even if I didn't entirely understand, I guessed that she was living in a world where there were no lies.

And while that hug lasted I was a happy mother.

Romain arrived later in the day, in time for the Yule log and the presents. He had a *girlfriend* with him. He drank low-alcohol Tourtel beers with his father and complained about them. This stuff is gnat's piss, he said, and Jo shut him up by saying nastily: Oh yeah? You go and ask Nadège what cheap plonk does to you, she'll tell you, you bloody idiot. The *girlfriend* yawned, and Christmas was spoilt. Nadine didn't say good-bye, she just went off into the cold, vanished into thin air. Romain finished the Yule log; he wiped his mouth with the back of his hand,

17

he licked his fingers and I wondered what was the point of all those years spent teaching him how to behave, to keep his elbows off the table, say thank you: all those lies. Before he left, he told us he was dropping out of his studies and going to work as a waiter, along with the *girl-friend*, at the Palais Breton, a crêperie in Uriage, the spa town ten minutes from Grenoble. I looked at my Jo; my eyes were telling him to do something, stop him, don't let him do this, but he just waved his bottle at our son the way men sometimes do in American films, wished him luck and that was that.

So there it is. I'm forty-seven years old.

Our children are living their own lives now. Jo hasn't left me for a younger, thinner, more beautiful woman yet. He works hard at the factory; they gave him a bonus last month, and if he does a training course, he's been told, he could be a foreman one day; being a foreman would bring him closer to his dreams.

His Cayenne, his flat-screen TV, his watch.

My own dreams have fled.

When I was ten and in Class CM2 at middle school, I dreamed of kissing Fabien Derôme, but it was Juliette Bocquet he kissed.

When I was thirteen, I danced to 'Indian Summer', and I prayed that my partner would put his hand on my brand-new breasts, but he didn't dare. After we finished the slow dance, I saw him laughing with his mates.

On my seventeenth birthday I dreamed that my mother would get up from the pavement where she'd fallen down all of a sudden, opening her mouth to utter a cry that never came. I dreamed that it wasn't true, not true, not true; that there wasn't a wet place between her legs all of a sudden, leaving a shameful damp patch on her dress. At seventeen I dreamed that my mother was immortal, would be able to help me make my wedding dress some day, advise me on the choice of my bouquet, the flavour of the wedding cake, the pale colour of the sugared almonds.

At twenty I dreamed of being a fashion designer, of going to Paris to train at the Studio Berçot or Esmod, but my father was already ill, so I took the job at Madame Pillard's haberdashery shop. At that age I dreamed in secret of Solal, of Prince Charming, of Johnny Depp and Kevin Costner before he had hair implants, but it was Jocelyn Guerbette, my stout Venantino Venantini, comfortably chubby and a charmer, who came along.

We first met in the haberdashery shop when he came in to buy something for his mother, thirty centimetres of Valenciennes lace, a bobbin lace made with continuous thread, very fine, with motifs worked into it: a miracle. You're the miracle, he told me. I blushed. My heart rose. He smiled. Men know the damage a few words can do to girls' hearts, and, idiots that we are, we swoon away and fall into the trap, excited because at last a man has set one for us.

He asked me out for a coffee after closing time. I'd dreamed a hundred times, a thousand times of the moment when a man would ask me out, pay court to me, want me. I'd dreamed of being abducted, carried away in a fast, purring car, forced on board a plane flying to islands. I'd dreamed of red cocktails, white fish, paprika and jasmine, not of a coffee at the newsagent and tobacconist's shop in the Arcades. Or a damp hand on mine. Or those clumsy words, unctuous phrases, already telling lies.

So that evening, after Jocelyn Guerbette had kissed me, starving and impatient as he was, after I had delicately fended him off and he had gone away promising to be back to see me next day, I opened my heart and let my dreams fly free.

I am happy with Jo.

He never forgets any of our anniversaries. He likes doing DIY in the garage at weekends. He makes small items of furniture that we sell at the flea market. Three months ago he installed WiFi for us because I'd decided to write a blog about my knitting. Sometimes, after a meal, he pinches my cheek and says, you're a good girl, Jo, you're a sweet girl. Yes, I know; he may sound a bit macho, but what he says comes from the heart. That's Jo for you.

He doesn't know much about delicacy, the light touch, the subtlety of words. He hasn't read many books; he'd rather have a quick run-down on a subject than a reasoned argument; he likes pictures better than writing. He loved the *Columbo* TV series because you knew who the killer was from the start.

I love words. I love long sentences, sighs that go on for ever. I love it when words sometimes hide what they're saying, or say it in a new way.

When I was young I kept a diary. I gave it up the day my mother died. When she collapsed my pen collapsed as well, and a lot of other things were broken.

So when we discuss something, Jo and I, I do most of the talking. He listens while he drinks his imitation beer; sometimes he nods to let me know that he understands and he's interested in my stories, and even if that's not true it's kind of him.

For my fortieth birthday he took a week's holiday from the factory, drove the children over to stay with his mother and we went to Étretat. We stayed half board at the Aiguille Creuse hotel, where we spent four wonderful days, and it seemed to me for the first time in my life that this was what being in love meant. We went for long walks on the cliffs, holding hands; sometimes, when there was no one else about, he pushed me up against the rocks, kissed me on the mouth and lost his hand down inside my panties. He used simple words to describe his desire. Called a spade a spade. *You make me hard. You excite me.* One evening at twilight on the Aval cliff I thanked him, I said, take me now, and he made love to me out of doors, fast and roughly; it was good. When we went back to the hotel our cheeks were flushed and our mouths dry, like a couple of tipsy teenagers, and it was a nice memory.

On Saturdays, Jo likes to go out with the guys from the factory. They play cards at the Café Georget, they talk man talk, sharing their dreams, sometimes whistling at girls the age of their own daughters, but they're nice guys;

it's *all talk and no action*, as we say; that's our menfolk for you.

In summer, the children go to stay with friends and Jo and I have three weeks in the south of the country at Villeneuve-Loubet. We stay on the Sourire campsite, and we get together with JJ and Marielle Roussel. We met them there by chance five years ago – they're from Dainville, only four kilometres from Arras! – and Michèle Henrion from Villeneuve-sur-Lot, the Agen prunes place, she's older than us, still an old maid. Jo claims it's because she sucks the prune stones when she should be sucking pricks. Pastis, barbecues, sardines; the beach at Cagnes opposite the hippodrome when it's very hot, Marineland once or twice, dolphins, seals, and then water-tobogganing, our screams of alarm that always turn to laughter, childish pleasures.

I'm happy with Jo.

It's not the life I dreamed of in my diary, when my mother was alive. My life isn't as perfect as the one she wished for me when she came to sit on the side of my bed in the evenings, when she stroked my hair gently, murmuring: You're an intelligent girl, Jo, you'll have a good life.

Even mothers tell lies. Because mothers are frightened too.

It's only in books that you can change your life. Wipe out everything at a stroke. Do away with the weight of things. Delete the nasty parts, and then at the end of a sentence suddenly find yourself on the far side of the world.

Danièle and Françoise have been playing the lottery for eighteen years. Every week they stake ten euros and dream of twenty million. A villa on the Côte d'Azur. A cruise round the world. Even just a trip to Tuscany. An island. A facelift. A diamond, a Santos Dumont ladies watch from Cartier. A hundred pairs of Louboutins and Jimmy Choos. A pink Chanel suit. Pearls, real pearls, the kind Jackie Kennedy wore, oh, wasn't she just lovely? They wait for the end of the week the way other people wait for the Messiah. Every Saturday their hearts are in their mouth as the balls go round. They hold their breath, they can't breathe. We could die at any moment! they cry in chorus.

Twelve years ago they won enough to open Coiff'Esthétique. They sent me a bunch of flowers every day while the building works went on, and we've been friends ever since, although I've developed a terrible allergy to flowers. They occupy the ground floor of a house that looks out over the Governor's garden in the Avenue des Fusillés. Françoise has almost been engaged several times, but the idea of abandoning her sister has always made her decide to abandon the idea of love instead; on the other hand, in 2003 Danièle went to live with a rep for L'Oréal shampoos, hair colours and other haircare products, a tall handsome man with raven-black hair and a baritone voice, very exotic. She had fallen for the wild odour of his skin, she'd been bowled over by the black hairs on the backs of his long fingers; Danièle had dreamed of animal lovemaking, of struggles and sexy wrestling, their flesh merging, but although the great ape had well-stocked balls, you couldn't deny that, he turned out to have a totally empty head – his ignorance was vast and positively tragic. The screwing was fine, she told me when she came back a month later, carrying her suitcase, it was screwing to die for, but after the screwing, that was it, the rep went to sleep and snored, then he was off again first thing in the morning on his hairy rounds, cultural level nil, and, said Danièle, whatever anyone says I do need to talk, I need to exchange ideas, we're not brute beasts, are we, no, we have souls!

The evening she came back we all went to have dinner at La Coupole, prawns on a bed of chicory for Françoise and me, Arras andouillettes for Danièle – there's no denying it, as far as I'm concerned making a break leaves a hole in me, Danièle said, a yawning gap, I have to fill it somehow – and after a bottle of wine the twins were in fits of laughter, promising never to leave each other again, or if one of them did meet Mr Right she would share him with the other.

Then they wanted to go dancing at the Copacabana club; they might find a couple of good-looking guys there, said one twin. Two Mr Rights, said the other, laughing. I didn't go with them.

I haven't gone dancing since that thirteenth birthday of mine when I danced to 'Indian Summer' with my budding breasts.

The twins disappeared into the night, taking their laughter and the slightly vulgar click-clack of their heels on the pavement with them, and I went home. I crossed the Boulevard de Strasbourg, I went up the Rue Gambetta to the Palais de Justice. A taxi passed, my hand trembled; I saw myself hailing it, climbing on board. I heard myself saying: Far away, please, as far away as possible. I saw the taxi drive off with me in the back, not turning round, not waving, not making any last gesture at all, with no regrets; I saw myself leaving, disappearing without a trace.

That was seven years ago.

But I went home instead.

Jo was asleep with his mouth open in front of the Radiola; a trickle of saliva shone on his chin. I switched off the TV. I put a blanket over his sprawled body. In his room Romain was fighting in the virtual world of Freelancer. In hers, Nadine was reading the conversations between Hitchcock and Truffaut; she was thirteen years old.

She raised her head when I opened the door of her room, she smiled at me and I thought how beautiful, how very beautiful she was. I loved her big blue eyes, I called them eyes full of the sky. I loved her clear skin, on which no injury had yet left any mark. I loved her silence and the smell of her skin. She moved up to the wall and said nothing when I lay down beside her.

Then she gently stroked my hair as my mother used to, and went on reading, out loud in a low voice this time, as grown-ups do to calm a small child's fears.

A journalist from *L'Observateur de l'Arrageois* came to the haberdashery shop this morning. She wanted to interview me about my *tengoldfingers* blog.

It's only a modest little thing.

I write every morning about the pleasures of knitting, embroidery and dressmaking. I've helped people to choose fabrics and wools; sequinned ribbons, velvet, satin and organdie; cotton lace and elastic; rat-tail cord, waxed shoelaces, braided rayon cord, anorak cords.

I sometimes write about the shop, a delivery of Velcro for sewing or tapes of press fasteners. I also send waves of nostalgia flowing out through the air to the embroiderers, lacemakers and weavers: their souls are the souls of women who wait. We are all like one of the Nathalies of *Eternal Return*, the Isolde figure in that film.

You already have over one thousand two hundred hits a day on your site, cries the journalist, one thousand two hundred, and that's just here, in the local area.

She's the age of a child you'd be proud of. She's pretty, with her freckles, her pink gums and white teeth.

Your blog is so unexpected. I have masses of questions to ask you. Why do one thousand two hundred women visit your site every day to talk about clothes? Why this sudden passion for knitting, dressmaking . . . the sense of touch? Do you think we suffer from a lack of physical contact these days? Has the virtual world killed off eroticism? I stop her. I don't know, I say, I don't know. Once people would have kept a private diary, now they write a blog. She tries again. Did you ever keep a diary? I smile. No. No, I never kept a diary, and I don't know the answers to any of your questions. I'm terribly sorry.

Then she puts down her notebook, her pencil, her bag.

She looks deep into my eyes. She puts her hand on mine, squeezes it and says: My mother's been living alone for over ten years. She gets up at six every morning. She makes herself a coffee. She waters her plants. She listens to the news on the radio. She drinks her coffee. She has a quick wash. An hour later, at seven, her day is over. Two months ago a neighbour told her about your blog, and she asked me to buy her *one of those thingummyjigs* – by a thingummyjig she meant a computer. And since then, thanks to your trimmings, your ribbon bows, your tie-backs for curtains, she's rediscovered the joys of life. So don't tell me you don't know any answers.

The journalist picked up her things, saying,

I'll be back, and then you'll have the answers.

It was eleven-twenty that morning when she left. My hands were trembling, my palms damp.

I shut the shop and went home.

I smiled when I looked at my teenage hand-writing again.

The dots over the letter *i* were circles, the letter *a* looked printed and the dots over the first *i* and the second *i* in the name of a boy called Philippe de Gouverne were tiny hearts.

Philippe de Gouverne. I remember him. He was the class intellectual. He was the funniest in the class, too. We teased him about the posh *de* in his name. We nicknamed him the Guvnor. I was madly in love with him. I thought he was so seductive, with a scarf that went twice round his neck and fell to his waist. When he was telling you something he used the ordinary past tense, and the music of his conjugation of verbs bewitched me. He used to say he was going to be a writer. Or a poet. He planned to write songs. In any case, he'd make the girls' hearts beat faster. Everyone laughed. Except for me.

But I never dared to approach him.

I turn the pages of my diary. Cinema tickets are stuck into it. A photograph of my first taste of flying on my seventh birthday, taken at Amiens-Glisy airport with Papa. He wouldn't remember it now. Since his stroke he's been living in the present. He has no past and no future. He lives in a present that lasts six minutes, and every six minutes the meter of his memory resets itself to zero. Every six minutes he asks me my name. Every six minutes he asks what day it is. Every six minutes he asks if Maman is coming to see him.

And then I find a sentence in violet ink near

the end of my diary, written before Maman collapsed on the pavement.

I'd like to have the chance to decide what my
life will be like, I think that's the best present
anyone can get.

The chance to decide what your life will be
like.

I close the diary. I'm grown-up now, so
I don't cry. I'm forty-seven years old with a
faithful, kind, sober husband; two grown-up
children and a little dead baby – I miss her
sometimes. I have a shop that, together with Jo's
salary, brings in enough each year for us to live a
pleasant life, nice holidays at Villeneuve-Loubet,
and – why not? – may yet allow us to make Jo's
wish for his dream car come true (I've seen a
second-hand one that struck me as good value
at thirty-six thousand euros). I write a blog that
makes the mother of a journalist on *L'Observateur
de l'Arrageois* happy every day, and probably one
thousand one hundred and ninety-nine other
ladies as well. And in view of the good figures
for my blog, the host site recently suggested

selling advertising space on it.

Jo makes me happy, and I've never wanted any other man, but all the same, you couldn't say I ever decided what my life would be like.

On my way back to the shop I'm crossing the Place des Héros when I hear my name being called. It's the twins. They're drinking coffee and filling in lottery tickets. Why don't you have a go for once, Françoise begs. You're not going to be a haberdasher all your life, are you? I tell her I like my shop. Don't you ever want to do something else? Danièle asks, backing up her sister. Have a go, come on!

So I go into the newsagent's and ask for a lottery ticket. Which? Which what? Lotto or EuroMillions? How would I know? Try EuroMillions, then, there's a good jackpot this Friday, says the newsagent. I give him the two euros he asks for, the machine picks the numbers and lucky stars for me, then he gives me a ticket. The twins applaud.

At last! Our little Jo will have lovely dreams tonight.

I slept very badly.

Jo was unwell all night. Diarrhoea and vomiting. He never complains of anything usually, but for some days now he's been saying he aches all over. He trembles the whole time – and not because of my kisses on his burning forehead, or the way I massage his chest to ease his cough, or because I sing Maman's nursery rhymes to soothe him.

The doctor came. It's probably the A/H1N1 virus, he says, that horrible swine flu. Yet they follow all the safety regulations at the factory. Face masks, hand-washing with alcohol gel, airing the workshops regularly, no handshaking, no kissing – and no screwing either, Jo added two days ago, before it struck him down. Dr Caron prescribed him Tamiflu and plenty of rest. That will be twenty-eight euros, Madame Guerbette.

Jo fell asleep in the morning. Although he had no appetite, I went to get two butter croissants, his favourite, at François Thierry's, I made a thermos flask of coffee and left it on his bedside table, just in case. I watched him sleeping for a little while. He was breathing noisily. Little beads of sweat kept forming at his temples, sliding down his cheeks, dropping on to his chest and dying there. I saw the new lines on his forehead, tiny wrinkles round his mouth like mini-brambles, the way his skin was beginning to slacken where it met his neck, just where he liked me to kiss him in our early days. I saw all those years of the past etched on his face, I saw time taking us further from our dreams and bringing us closer to silence. I thought my Jo looked good, sleeping like a sick child, and I liked the lie I had told myself. I thought that if the most handsome man in the world, the kindest man, the most *everything* man appeared right here and now I wouldn't get up, I wouldn't follow him, I wouldn't even smile at him.

I'd stay here, because Jo needs me, and a woman needs to be needed.

The most handsome man in the world doesn't need anything because he already has everyone and everything. He has his handsome looks, and the irrepressible, insatiable desire of all the women who want to feast on them and will end up devouring him and leaving him for dead, bones sucked dry, brilliant and white in the pit of their vanity.

Later I called Françoise. She said she'd tape a notice to my shop window. *Closed for two days on account of flu.* Then I posted the news on my blog.

A hundred emails arrived within the hour.

People offering to run the shop for me while my husband recovered. People asking me Jo's size, so that they could knit him sweaters, gloves, caps. People wanting to know if I needed any help, blankets, someone to be with me, help out with cooking and housework, a friend to talk to at this difficult time. It was incredible. My *tengoldfingers* blog had opened up buried, forgotten stores of kindness. My anecdotes about cords, drawstrings and decorative thread seemed to have created a strong bond within a whole invisible community of women who, in rediscovering the pleasures of sewing, had suddenly replaced the loneliness of their lives with the joy of being part of a family.

Someone rang the doorbell.

It was a neighbour, an adorable dried-up little twig of a woman who looks like the actress Madeleine Renaud. She was bringing me some tagliatelle. I coughed – so much unexpected solicitude had me all choked up. I wasn't used to being given something I hadn't even asked for. I couldn't speak. She smiled so sweetly.

They're made with spinach and fromage frais.
Carbohydrates and iron. You need to keep your
strength up, Jo. I stammered thanks, and my
tears poured out, I couldn't help it.

I went to see my father.

After asking who I was, he wanted news of Maman. I told him she was shopping, she'd look in a little later. I hope she'll bring me my newspaper, he said, and some shaving foam, I've run out.

I talked to him about the shop, and he asked me for the hundredth time if I owned it. He couldn't get over it, he was so proud of me. *Jo's Haberdashery, formerly Maison Pillard. Jo's Haberdashery*, your name on a shop sign, Jo, fancy that! I'm so pleased for you. Then he raised his head and looked at me. Who are you?

Who are you? Our six minutes were up.

Jo was better. The Tamiflu, rest, the tagliatelle with spinach and fromage frais had got the better of his nasty flu. He stayed at home for several days doing a bit of DIY, and when he opened a Tourtel low-alcohol beer and switched the TV on one evening, I knew he was back to normal again. Life went on as usual, calm and quiet.

In the following days, however, the haberdashery shop was never empty, and *tengoldfingers* now had over five thousand hits a day. For the first time in twenty years I ran out of casein, corozo and bakelite buttons, cutwork and bobbin lace, cross-stitch and sampler patterns as well as pompons. Or rather *the* pompon, the only one in stock, because I hadn't sold any pompons for a year. I felt as if I were in the middle of a soppy Frank Capra film, and I can tell you that a bit of slush sometimes feels really good.

When all that died down, Danièle, Françoise and I did up parcels of the blankets, sweaters and embroidered pillowcases that kind people had sent for Jo, and Danièle said she would take them to a charity shop run by the diocese of Arras.

But the most important event in that period of our lives, the one that sent the twins into a two-day fit of hysterics, was the fact that the winning EuroMillions ticket had been sold in Arras. In Arras, good heavens, the arse-end of nowhere, it could have been us! they cried. Eighteen million euros, so OK, not a huge win like the seventy-five million won on a ticket bought in Franconville, but all the same, eighteen million! In the arse-end of nowhere!

What sent them into even more of a flat spin, indeed left them practically apoplectic, was the fact that the holder of the winning ticket still hadn't turned up.

And now there were only four days left before the win was lost and the money went back into the jackpot.

I don't know how I knew, but I did.

I knew, even without looking at the numbers, that it was me.

One chance in seventy-six million, and it happened to me. I read the framed box showing the numbers in the *Voix du Nord*. They were all there.

The 6, the 7, the 24, the 30, the 32. And lucky stars 4 and 5.

A ticket bought in Arras in the Place des Héros. For a stake of two euros. Picked at random.

18,547,301 euros and 28 centimes.
I felt faint.

Jo found me on the kitchen floor – just as I'd found Maman on the pavement thirty years ago.

We were setting out to go shopping together when I realised that I'd left our shopping list on the kitchen table. I went back for it while Maman waited for me outside.

When I went out again, at the very moment when I was stepping out into the street, I saw her looking at me with her mouth wide open, but no sound came out; her face was twisted, grimacing like the face of the horrible person in Munch's picture *The Scream*, and she folded in on herself like an accordion. I lost my mother within four seconds. I ran to her, but it was too late.

When someone's dying, you always run to that person too late. As if by chance.

There were people shouting, the sound of a car braking. Words seemed to be flowing out of my mouth like tears, stifling me.

Then the damp patch appeared on her dress between her legs. It grew visibly, like a shameful tumour. I immediately felt the cold of a wing-beat in my throat, the heat of a scratching claw, and then, like the mouth of the person in the painting, like my mother's mouth, mine opened, and a bird flew out from between my grotesque lips. In the open air it let out a terrifying cry; its chilling song.

A song of death.

Jo panicked. He thought I had that dreadful flu. He wanted to call Dr Caron, but I came back to my senses and reassured him. It's nothing, I said, I didn't have time for any lunch. Help me to get up, I'll sit down for five minutes and then I'll be all right, I'll be fine. You're so hot, he said, feeling my forehead. I'll be fine, I tell you, and anyway I'm having my period, that's why I'm hot.

Period. The magic word. It puts most men off.

I'll warm up something for you, he suggested, opening the fridge. Unless you'd rather order a pizza. I smiled. My Jo. My dear Jo. Or we could eat out for once, I murmured. He smiled and got himself a Tourtel. I'll put on a jacket, my beauty, and then I'm your man.

We ate at the Vietnamese restaurant two streets away. There was hardly anyone there, and I wondered how the place kept going. I ordered a light soup with rice noodles (*bun than*), Jo ordered fried fish (*cha ca*), and I took his hand in mine the way I used to when we were engaged twenty years ago. Your eyes are shining, he whispered with a nostalgic smile.

And if you could hear my heart beating, I

thought, you'd be afraid it was going to explode.

Our orders arrived quite quickly. I hardly touched my soup, and Jo looked anxious. Are you sure you're all right? I cast down my eyes.

There's something I have to tell you, Jo.

He must have sensed that it was impor-tant. He put his chopsticks down and wiped his lips with the cotton napkin – he always made an effort in a restaurant – and took my hand. His dry lips were shaking. Tell me it's nothing serious? You're not ill, are you, Jo? Because . . . because if anything happened to you it would be the end of the world . . . Tears came to my eyes, and at the same time I began laughing, a restrained laugh that sounded like happiness. I'd die without you, Jo. No, Jo, it's nothing serious. Don't worry, I whispered. I just wanted to tell you I love you.

And I swore to myself that no sum of money would be worth losing all this for.

We made love very gently that night.

Was it because of my pallor, my new fragility? Was it because of the unreasonable fear he'd had of losing me a few hours earlier in the restaurant? Was it because we hadn't made love for quite a while, and he needed time to relearn the geography of desire, tame his masculine forcefulness? Was it because he loved me enough to rate my pleasure above his own?

That night I didn't know. I do know now. But oh God, it was a beautiful night.

It brought to mind the first nights lovers spend together, nights when you'd be happy to die at dawn, nights that care only for themselves, far from the world, its noise, its nastiness. And then, as time goes on, the noise and nastiness come your way and it is difficult to wake up, the disillusionment is cruel. Desire is always followed by boredom. And only love can defeat boredom. Love with a capital L; we all dream of it.

I remember crying at the end of Albert Cohen's novel *Belle du Seigneur*. I even felt angry when the lovers threw themselves out of the window of the Ritz in Geneva. I threw my own copy of the book in the rubbish bin, and in its brief fall it took the capital L away with it.

But that night it seemed to have come back.

At dawn Jo went out. For the last month he'd been on a course from seven-thirty to nine every morning, in order to become a foreman and get closer to his dreams.

But now, my love, I thought, I can make your dreams come true; they don't cost as much as all that. A flat-screen Sony 52-inch TV set: 1,400 euros. A Seiko watch: 400 euros. A new fireplace in the sitting room: 500 euros plus 1,500 euros for fitting it. A Porsche Cayenne: 89,000 euros. And your complete set of James Bond films, all 22 of them: 170 euros.

This is dreadful. I'm thinking I hardly know what.

Whatever's happening to me, it scares me silly.

I have an appointment at the French Gaming headquarters in Boulogne-Billancourt, up in Paris.

I caught an early train this morning. I told Jo I had to see my suppliers Synextile, Eurotessile and Filagil Sabarent. I'll be home late, I told him, don't wait up for me, there's a chicken breast in the fridge and some ratatouille that you can warm up.

He went to the station with me and then hurried to the factory, to get there in time for his training course.

In the train I think of the twins' dreams, their disappointment every Friday evening when the balls fall and the numbers on them are not the numbers that Françoise and Danièle have chosen so carefully, thinking hard about them, assessing them, weighing them up.

I think of the readers of *tengoldfingers*, those five thousand Princess Auroras who dream of pricking their finger on the spindle of a spinning wheel, going to sleep and being woken by a kiss.

I think of Papa's six-minute loops of time. Of the vanity of everything. Of what money can never make up for.

I think of all that Maman didn't have, the things she dreamed of that I could now give her: a trip up the Nile, a Saint Laurent jacket, a cleaning lady, a Kelly bag, a ceramic crown for her tooth instead of the horrible gold one that spoilt her wonderful smile, an apartment in the Rue des Teinturiers, an evening in Paris at the Moulin Rouge and the Brasserie Mollard with its delicious oysters, grandchildren. She used to say, grandmothers make the best mothers, a mother has too much to do to be a woman. I miss my mother as much as I did on the day she collapsed. I feel sad whenever I think of her. I always cry. Who must I give the money to so that she can come back, all eighteen million five hundred and forty-seven thousand, three hundred and one euros and twenty-eight centimes of it?

I think of myself, of all that will now be possible for me, and I don't want any of it. I don't want what all the money in the world can buy. But does everyone feel like that?

When I arrive, the receptionist is charming.

Ah, so you're the one who bought the ticket in Arras. And she asks me to wait in a small sitting room, offers me magazines to read, a tea or a coffee. I say: No thank you, I've already drunk three coffees this morning, and at once I feel stupid and provincial, a real idiot. A little later she comes back and takes me to the office of a man called Hervé Meunier, who welcomes me with open arms.

Well, you certainly had us worried, he says, laughing, but here you are at last, that's the main thing. Sit down, please. Make yourself comfortable, we want you to feel at home. My new home is a big office with a thick carpet; I unobtrusively slip off one of my flat-heeled shoes to let my foot stroke the pile, sink a little way into it. Gentle air conditioning keeps the temperature comfortable, and outside the windows there are other big office blocks. They look like huge pictures, Hoppers in black and white.

This is the point of departure for new lives. Here, face to face with Hervé Meunier, people receive the talisman that will change everything for them.

The Holy Grail.

A cheque made out in their name. A cheque made out to Jocelyne Guerbette, for the sum of 18,547,301 euros 28 centimes.

He asks me for the lottery ticket and my ID. He checks them. He makes a short phone call. The cheque will be ready in a few minutes' time – would you like a coffee? We have the entire

Nespresso range. This time I don't say anything. Just as you please. Personally I'm hooked on the Livanto blend because of its smooth, rounded, velvety aroma. Well, while we're waiting, he goes on, I'd like you to meet a colleague of mine. In fact, you *must* meet my colleague.

The colleague is a psychologist. I didn't know that having eighteen million euros was an illness. But I make no comment.

The psychologist turns out to be a woman. She looks like Emmanuelle Béart; like her, she has Daisy Duck lips, lips so swollen, says my Jo, that they'd explode if she bit them. She is wearing a black suit that emphasises her plastic look (as in plastic surgery), she offers me a bony hand and says this won't take long. In fact it takes her forty minutes to explain that what's happened to me is both a stroke of good luck and a great misfortune. I'm rich. I'll be able to buy anything I want. But I must tread carefully. I mustn't be too trusting. Because when you have money, she explains, all of a sudden people love you. Total strangers love you. They'll ask you to marry them. They'll send you poems. Love letters. Hate letters. They'll ask you for money to nurse a little girl whose name is Jocelyne, like yours, and who has leukaemia. They'll send you pictures of an ill-treated dog and ask you to be its godmother, its saviour; they'll promise you a kennel in your name, dog biscuits, dog food, a dog show. The mother of a child with a muscle-wasting disease will send you an upsetting video of her little boy falling in a stairwell and hitting his head on the wall, and ask you for money to install a lift in their apartment block. Another woman will send you photos of her own mother dribbling and incontinent, and ask you with grief-stricken tears to help pay for her to have a nurse at home. She'll even send you a form so that you can deduct tax from your donation. A woman called Guerbette living in Pointe-à-Pitre in Guadeloupe will discover that she's your cousin, and ask you for the money for an air fare so that she can come and see you, and then money for a studio flat, and then more money so that she can bring over a friend who's a healer and will help you to lose those extra kilos. And I haven't even mentioned the bankers. Sugary-sweet, all of a sudden. Madame Guerbette here, bowing and scraping there. I have tax-exempt investments for you, they'll say, invest overseas, invest in the tax-deductible restoration of old buildings as specified in the Malraux Law, invest in fine wines. In gold, in property, in precious stones. They won't mention the wealth taxes. Fiscal controls. Or their own fees.

I know the illness the psychologist is talking about. It's the illness that afflicts people who don't win, they're trying to inoculate me with their own fears like a vaccine against evil. I protest. Some people have survived, after all. And I've only won eighteen million. What about people who have won a hundred, fifty, even thirty million? Exactly, replies the psychologist, looking mysterious, exactly.

Now, and only now, do I accept a coffee. I think the blend is Livato, or Livatino maybe, a well-rounded flavour, in any case. With one sugar, thank you. There have been many suicides, she tells me. Many, many cases of depression, many divorces, much hatred and tragedy. We've heard of knife wounds. Injuries from shower-heads. Burns inflicted with butane gas cylinders. Families torn apart, destroyed. Deceitful daughters-in-law, alcoholic sons-in-law. Contract killers, just like in bad films. I knew of one step-father who promised one thousand five hundred euros to anyone who would eliminate his wife, she said. She'd won a little less than seventy thousand euros. A son-in-law who cut off two fingers to get a credit-card code. Forged signatures, forged documents. Money drives people mad, Madame Guerbette, it's behind four out of five crimes. One out of two cases of depression. I have no advice to give you, she concludes, only this information. We have a psychological support service if you would like to make use of it. She puts down her coffee cup; she hasn't so much as moistened her Daisy Duck lips with the drink. Have you told your close family? No, I say. Excellent, she says. We can help you to break the news to them, find words to minimise the shock, because believe me, it will be a shock. Do you have children? I nod. Well, they won't just see you as a mother now, they'll see you as a rich mother and they'll want their share. And then there's your husband; let's suppose he has an ordinary kind of job. He'll want to give it up and devote himself to managing *your* fortune, I say yours because from now on it will be his as well since he loves you, oh yes, he'll tell you how much he loves you in the days and months to come, he'll give you flowers — here I interrupt her to say I'm allergic to flowers — he'll give you . . . give you chocolates, give you I don't know what, she goes on, but anyway he'll spoil you, he'll lull you into a false sense of security, he'll poison you. Because this is a script written in advance, Madame Guerbette, written long ago, greed burns everything in its path. Think of the Borgias, the Agnellis, or more recently the Bettencourt family.

Then she makes me assure her that I've taken in everything she's said. She gives me a small business card with four emergency numbers on it. Don't hesitate to call us, Madame Guerbette, and don't forget, from now on you're not going to be loved for yourself alone. Then she takes me back to Hervé Meunier's office.

He is smiling broadly, flashing his teeth.

Those teeth remind me of the teeth of the salesman who sold Jo and me our first used car, a blue 1983 Ford Escort, one Sunday in March in the Leclerc shopping-centre car park. It was raining.

Your cheque, says Hervé Meunier. Eighteen million five hundred and forty-seven thousand, three hundred and one euros and twenty-eight centimes, he announces slowly, as if reading out a sentence in court. Are you sure you wouldn't prefer a bank transfer?

'I'm sure.'

The fact is, I'm not sure of anything now.

My train for Arras leaves in seven hours' time.

I could always ask Hervé Meunier, since he has suggested it, to get my ticket changed and have a seat reserved on an earlier train, but it's a fine day. I'd like to walk for a while. I need some fresh air. Daisy Duck has delivered me a knock-out blow. I can't believe that there's a murderer, or even a liar, still less a thief inside my Jo. Or that my children will look at me with eyes like Uncle Scrooge McDuck's in the comics I read as a child – big, greedy eyes with dollar signs leaping out of them whenever he saw something he wanted.

Greed burns everything in its path, she said.

Hervé Meunier goes out to the street with me. He wishes me luck. You look like a good person, Madame Guerbette. A good person, my foot. A person in possession of eighteen million euros, yes. A fortune that all his ingratiating ways will never bring him. It's odd how servants often give the impression of owning their masters' wealth. Sometimes with such brilliant skill that you let yourself become *their* servant. Servant of the servant. Don't make too much of it, Monsieur Meunier, I say, withdrawing my hand, which he is holding with damp persistence in his own. He lowers his eyes and goes back into the building, opens the revolving door with a swipe card. He's returning to his office where none of the fixtures and fittings belong to him, not even the thick carpet or the vista of office blocks like pictures on the wall. He's like those bank clerks who count thousands of notes that only burn their fingers.

Until a certain day comes.

I go back up the Rue Jean-Jaurès to the Boulogne-Jean Jaurès metro station, line 8 going in the direction of the Gare d'Austerlitz, and change at La Motte-Picquet. I look at my piece of paper. Take line 8 towards Créteil-Préfecture and get out at La Madeleine, cross the Boulevard de la Madeleine, go down the Rue Duphot and up the Rue Cambon on my left to number 31.

I hardly have time to put out my hand before the door is opening as if of its own accord, thanks to a doorman. Two steps and I'm in another world. The air is cool. The lighting is soft. The salesgirls are beautiful and discreet; one of them comes over to me and whispers, Can I help you, madame? Just looking, just looking, I murmur, impressed, but she's the one who's looking at me.

My grey coat is old, but incredibly comfortable, my flat shoes – I chose them early this morning because my feet swell in the train – my shapeless, well-worn bag . . . she smiles at me.

Don't hesitate to ask me anything you'd like to know. She moves away, discreetly elegant.

I go over to look at a pretty cotton and linen tweed jacket in two colours: 2,490 euros. The twins would love it. I ought to buy two: that would come to 4,980 euros. A lovely pair of PVC sandals with 90 mm heels: 1,950 euros. Tapered fingerless lambskin gloves: 650 euros. A very simple white ceramic watch: 3,100 euros. A beautiful crocodile bag, Maman would have loved one like that but would never have dared to carry it: price on application.

Where does a price on application start?

Suddenly an actress whose name I can never remember makes her way out of the boutique. She is carrying a large bag in each of her hands. She passes so close to me that I can smell her perfume, something heavy, slightly nauseating, vaguely sexy. The doorman bows to her, but she takes no notice. Outside, her chauffeur hurries to take the bags. She dives into a large black car and disappears, swallowed up behind the darkened glass.

What a fuss!

I could do that too – I, Jocelyne Guerbette, the Arras haberdasher. I could ransack the Chanel boutique, hire a chauffeur and go about in a limousine, but what for? The loneliness I'd seen in that woman's face frightened me. So I discreetly leave the dreamy boutique, the sales-girl gives me a politely regretful smile, the door-man opens the door but doesn't bow to me, or if he does I don't notice.

Outside, the air is keen. The sound of car horns, the threat of impatience, drivers' desire to murder each other, the kamikaze messengers in the Rue de Rivoli a dozen or so metres away – all that suddenly seems reassuring. No more thick carpet, no more oily bowing and scraping. Just plain ordinary violence. Petty pain. Sadness that doesn't go away. Strong smells, vaguely animal and chemical, the sort you get just beyond the station at Arras. My real life.

I make for the Jardin des Tuileries, clutching my ugly bag, my safe, to my stomach; Jo told me to watch out for the lowlife of Paris. There are gangs of kids who'll rob you blind before you notice a thing. Women begging with newborn babies who never cry, can hardly move because they're knocked out with denoral or hexapneumine. I think of Hieronymus Bosch's *The Magician*. Maman loved that picture, she knew every detail of it, like the nutmegs on the swindler's table.

I go back up the Allée de Diane to the north portico, where I sit down on a small stone bench. There's a puddle of sunlight at my feet. All of a sudden I'd like to be Thumbelina. Plunge into that golden pool. Warm myself in it. Burn in it.

Oddly enough, even surrounded by cars and horrible scooters, jammed between the Rue de Rivoli and the Quai Voltaire, the particles of air look cleaner and clearer to me. I know that's not possible. It's the product of my imagination, of my fear. I take my sandwich out of my bag; Jo made it for me this morning, when it was still dark outside. Two slices of bread and butter, tuna and hard-boiled egg between them. I said, Oh no, don't bother, I'll buy something at the station. But he insisted. They're all thieves, especially at railway stations, they'll sell you a sandwich for eight euros and it won't be as good as mine. You can't even be sure it's fresh.

My Jo. So thoughtful. Your sandwich is really good, Jo.

A few metres away there's a statue of Apollo in hot pursuit of Daphne, and another of Daphne pursued by the very same Apollo. Further off there's a callipygous Venus; *callipygous*, adjective. I remember finding out its definition during drawing lessons: having a beautiful bottom. Meaning big, fat. Like mine. And here I am, Jocelyne from Arras, sitting on my beautiful bottom and eating a sandwich in the Jardin des Tuileries like a student, while carrying a fortune around in my bag.

A terrifying fortune, because I suddenly realise that Jo is right.

Even at eight euros, twelve, fifteen, no sandwich would be as good as the one he made me.

Later, and I still have time before my train

leaves, I forage about in the Marché Saint-Pierre, the big textiles market in the Rue Charles Nodier. This is my Ali Baba cave.

My hands plunge into the fabrics, my fingers tremble at the contact with organdie, fine felt, jute, patchwork. I feel the intoxication that must have been felt by that woman who was shut up all night in the Sephora cosmetics store in their lovely advertising film. All the gold in the world wouldn't buy you that dizzying feeling. All the women here are beautiful. Their eyes shine. Looking at a piece of fabric, they already imagine a dress, a cushion, a doll. They make dreams; they have the beauty of the world at their fingertips. Before I leave I buy some Bemberg lining, some polypropylene webbing, cotton rickrack braid and beaded pompons.

My happiness costs less than forty euros.

I spend the fifty minutes of the journey back to Arras dozing in the hushed atmosphere of the high-speed train. I wonder whether Romain and Nadine will want anything, now that I can provide it. Romain could open his own crêperie.

Nadine could make as many films as she likes and not have to depend on their success to live comfortably. But will that make up for the time we haven't spent together? Holidays far apart from each other, going short of things, hours of cold and solitude? Fears?

Does money cut distances short, bring people together?

And what about you, Jo, what would you do if you knew about all this? Tell me, what would you do?

Jo was waiting for me at the station.

As soon as he saw me he quickened his pace without actually breaking into a run. He took me in his arms on the platform. This unexpected show of emotion surprised me; I laughed, almost embarrassed. Jo, Jo, what's all this about? Jo, he murmured in my ear. I'm so glad to see you back.

There we are.

The bigger the lie, the less we see it coming.

He let go of me, his hand slipped into mine

and we walked home together. I told him about my day. I quickly invented a meeting at Filagil Sabarent, the textiles wholesale firm in the 3rd arrondissement. I showed him the wonderful things I'd bought in the Marché Saint-Pierre.

And what about my sandwich? Was it a good sandwich? he asked. I stood on tiptoe and kissed his throat. The best in the world, I said. Like you.

F rançoise rushed into my shop.

   Guess what! she cried. She's gone to collect her cheque! It's a woman. It says so in the *Voix du Nord*, a woman from Arras who wants to remain anonymous! There, look! Do you realise, she waited till the last minute! I'd have gone off right away, I'd have been so scared they might not pay me the eighteen million. Think about it, Jo – OK, so it's not as much as the hundred million won by a ticket in Venelles, but that was a syndicate of fifteen people, they got six million each, while this woman won eighteen million all to herself, eighteen million, over a thousand years of work at the minimum hourly rate, Jo, a thousand years, just think! Danièle arrived as well. She was red in the face and carrying three coffees. Oh, my goodness, she breathed, what a thing! I looked in at the newsagent's, no one knows who it is, not even that sly shampoo girl at Jean-Jac's. Françoise interrupted her. We'll soon see a Maserati or a Cayenne around the place, then we'll know who she is. No, those aren't the kind of cars a woman would buy. More likely a Mini or a Fiat 500.

Or perhaps she won't buy a car at all, I interrupt, killjoy that I am. Perhaps she won't change anything in her life.

The twins laughed heartily. Because you wouldn't change anything, is that it? You'd stay here in your little haberdashery shop, selling odds and ends to keep bored women occupied, women who aren't even brave enough to take lovers? said Danièle. No, you wouldn't! You'd do the same as us, you'd change your life, you'd buy a lovely house by the sea, maybe in Greece, you'd go for a wonderful holiday, buy yourself a nice car, spoil your children – and your friends, added Danièle. You'd get a new wardrobe, you'd go round the Paris boutiques, you wouldn't think twice about the expense, and, well, if you felt guilty you could always make a donation to cancer research. Or multiple sclerosis, or whatever. I shrugged my shoulders. I can do that without winning the lottery, I said. Yes, but it's not the same thing, they replied. Not the same thing at all. You can't . . .

A customer came in, and that shut us up; made us stifle our laughter.

She looked without much interest at handles for bags, tried the feel of one in her hand, then she turned round and asked me how Jo was now. I reassured her and thanked her.

I hope he liked my waistcoat, she said. The green one with wooden buttons. And then she started to sob and told me that her grown-up daughter was in hospital dying of the horrible flu that was going round. I don't know what to do, what to say to her. You use such lovely words in your blog, Jo, what can I say to her when I say goodbye? Can you give me some words? Please.

Danièle and Françoise disappeared. Even if they'd had eighteen million euros, even if we'd all had eighteen million euros, still we'd have nothing, face to face with this mother.

When we got to the hospital, her grown-up daughter had been moved to intensive care.

I'd hidden the cheque under the insole of an old shoe.

Sometimes, at night, I'd wait for Jo to start snoring before getting out of bed, tiptoeing over to the wardrobe, putting my hand into my shoe and taking out the paper treasure. Then I'd lock myself in the bathroom, sit down on the lavatory lid, unfold the cheque and look at it.

The figures made my head spin.

On my eighteenth birthday, Papa had given me the equivalent of two thousand five hundred euros. That's a lot of money, he'd said. You could use it to pay the deposit on an apartment, you could take a nice holiday, you could buy all the books on fashion you want, or a little second-hand car if you'd prefer that. And I had felt rich. I realise now that I was rich in his confidence, which is the greatest wealth of all.

A cliché, I know. But it is true.

Before he had the stroke that has imprisoned him ever since in a loop of six minutes of the present, he worked for over twenty years in the ADMC, the chemicals factory in Tilloy-lès-Mofflaines, four kilometres from Arras. He supervised the manufacture of didecyl ammonium chloride and glutaraldehyde. Maman made sure that he took a shower as soon as he got home. Papa smiled, and accepted her insistence with good grace. While glutaraldehyde was indeed soluble in water, the same couldn't be said of didecyl ammonium chloride. But the tomatoes we grew never turned blue, our eggs did not explode and no tentacles grew on our backs. Obviously good Marseille soap worked miracles.

Maman taught drawing to primary-school classes, and took a life class at the Museum of Fine Art on Wednesday evenings. She had a wonderful way with a pencil. Our family did not have a photo album but a notebook full of drawings. My childhood was like a work of art. Maman was beautiful, and Papa loved her.

I look at that damn cheque, and I can sense it looking back at me.

Accusing me.

I know that you can never do enough for your parents, and by the time you're aware of that it's too late. To Romain, I'm only a phone number stored in his mobile, some memories of holidays in Bray-Dunes and a few Sundays at the Bay of Somme. He doesn't indulge me, just as I didn't indulge my parents. We always pass on our faults. With Nadine it's different. She doesn't talk, she gives. It's up to us to decipher her message. To receive it. Since last Christmas she's been sending me her little films from London over the Internet.

The latest is a minute long.

There's only one shot, and some rather violent zoom effects. You see an old woman standing on a platform at Victoria Station. She has white hair; it looks like a big snowball. She's just got out of a train, she takes a few steps and then puts down her case, which is too heavy. She looks around her; the crowd bypasses her like water flowing round a pebble, and suddenly she's all alone, tiny, forgotten. The woman is not an actress. The crowd is not a crowd of extras. It's a real image. Real people. A real story. An ordinary defeat. As background music, Nadine has chosen the *adagietto* from Mahler's Fifth Symphony, and she has made that minute the most moving minute I've ever had the privilege of seeing; it says everything about the pain of abandonment. Loss. Fear. Death.

I fold up the cheque, suppressing it in my clenched fist.

I'm beginning to lose weight.

I think it's stress. I don't go home in the middle of the day any more, I stay at the shop and I skip lunch. The twins are worried. I tell them I'm behind with my accounts, I have orders to deal with, and then there's my blog. It gets almost eight thousand hits a day now. I agreed to have advertising on the blog, so I can pay Mado with the money that brings in. Since her grown-up daughter died of pneumonia in intensive care last month, Mado has had time on her hands. She has too many words now. Too much love left over. She's brimming over with useless information, recipes she'll never cook again (a leek tart, brown-sugar biscuits), nursery rhymes for the grandchildren she'll never have. She still cries sometimes in the middle of a sentence, or when she hears a song, or when a girl comes in and asks for some twill or grosgrain ribbon for her mother. She's working here these days. She replies to the messages left on *tengoldfingers*; she takes orders and sends the stuff out now that we have a mini-sales site. Her grown-up daughter was called Barbara. She was the same age as Romain.

Mado loves the twins; they're crazy, she says, but they have such *oomph*, such get-up-and-go! She's trying to bring her vocabulary up to date now that she helps me with the blog.

That's what I call chutzpah!

Every Wednesday she goes to have lunch with Danièle and Françoise at the Deux Frères in the Rue de la Taillerie. They order a salad, Perrier water, sometimes a glass of wine, but most important of all they fill in their lottery tickets. They search their memory for lucky numbers. An anniversary. The date of an amorous encounter. Their ideal weight. Their social-security numbers. The numbers of the houses they grew up in. The date of a first kiss. The date, never to be forgotten, when inconsolable grief struck. A telephone number that never replies any more.

Every Wednesday afternoon, when Mado comes back, her eyes are shining and as round as lottery balls. And every Wednesday afternoon she says, Oh, Jo, Jo, if I won, if I were to win, you've no idea of all the things I'd do!

And today, for the first time, I ask her, What *would* you do, Mado? I don't quite know, she replies. But it would be extraordinary.

It was today that I began my list.

L ist of the things I need.

A lamp for the hall table.

A coat-and-hatstand (bistro-style).

*A board to hold keys and the post (from Cash
    Express?).*

Two Tefal saucepans.

A new microwave.

A vegetable rack.

A bread knife.

A potato peeler.

Dusters.

A couscous steamer.

Two sets of sheets for our bedroom.

A duvet and duvet cover.

A non-slip mat to go in the bath.

A shower curtain (not flowery!).

A small medicine cupboard (for the bathroom wall).

A magnifying mirror with a built-in light. (Saw it on the Internet, made by Babyliss. 62.56 euros plus delivery.)

A new pair of tweezers.

Slippers for Jo.

Quiès earplugs (because one of us snores!).

A small rug for Nadine's room.

A new handbag (Chanel? Look at Dior too).

A new coat. (Go back to Caroll's in the Rue Rouille for another look. Pretty coat there, 30% wool, 70% alpaca. Very comfortable. Has a slimming effect. 330 euros.)

A BlackBerry (because of the blog).

A train ticket to London. (With Jo. Two days there at least.)

A small radio for the kitchen.

A new ironing board.

An iron (saw a very nice Calor steam turbo in Auchan, 300.99 euros).

Intensive treatment and repair mask for my hair. (Marionnaud, 2.90 euros and 10.20 euros respectively.)

Belle du Seigneur. (To reread. Saw Folio edition in Brunet.)

Copy of Les finances personnelles pour les Nuls.

Underpants and socks for Jo.

A flat-screen TV. (???)

All the James Bond films on DVD. (???)

The journalist is back.

Bringing croissants and a little tape recorder. I can't wriggle out of it.

No, I don't know how it all began. Yes, I wanted to share my passion. No, I never really thought so many women would be interested. No, *tengoldfingers* is not for sale. I don't do it for the money. No, I don't think money can buy that sort of thing. Yes, it's true that I make some money from the advertising. It means I can pay a salary to Mado, who helps me.

Yes, I enjoy it and yes, I'm proud of it. No, it hasn't gone to my head, and no again, you can't really call it a success. Yes, success is dangerous when you stop doubting yourself. Oh yes, I doubt myself every day. No, my husband doesn't help with the blog. He does help me think about what we stock for the site, yes, because sales are going well; we even sent a cross-stitch kit to Moscou yesterday. What, Moscow in Russia? I laugh. No, the Moscou that's a district in Toulouse near the Canal du Midi. Oh, that one. No, there's no message in what I'm doing. Only pleasure, and patience. Yes, I do think that not everything from the past is outmoded. Giving yourself a chance to possess something very good, taking your time, that's important. Yes, I think everything does go too fast these days. We talk too fast. We think too fast – if we think at all, that is! We send emails and texts without reading them through, we lose the elegance of proper spelling, politeness, the sense of things. I've seen children publish pictures of themselves vomiting on Facebook. No, no, I'm not against progress; I'm just afraid it will isolate people even more. Last month there was a news item about a young girl who wanted to die, she told her 237 Facebook friends in advance and no one reacted. What did you say? Yes, she's dead. She hanged herself. No one told her that it would mean twenty minutes of atrocious pain. That suicides always want to be saved, but only silence answers their suffocated pleas. Well, since you want a formula so badly I'll say that *tengoldfingers* is like the fingers of a hand. Women are the fingers and the hand is their passion. Can she quote me on that? No, no, it sounds ridiculous. On the contrary, she thinks it's touching. A pretty comparison.

Then she turns off her tape recorder.

I think I've got lots of wonderful stuff for my article, thank you, Jo. Oh, one last question. You must have heard about the woman from Arras who won eighteen million in the lottery? Suddenly I am wary. Yes. If it was you, Jo, what would you do with it? I don't know what to say. Would you expand *tengoldfingers*? she goes on.

Help women living alone? Set up a foundation?

I start stammering. I . . . I don't know. Anyway . . . anyway, that's purely theoretical. And I'm not a saint, you know. I live a simple life, and I like it that way.

Thank you very much, Jo.

'Papa, I've won eighteen million euros.'

Papa looks at me. He can't believe his ears. His mouth opens in a smile, which turns to laughter. Nervous laughter at first, turning to joy. He wipes away the little tears that spring to his eyes. That's wonderful, my little girl, you must be pleased. Have you told Maman? Yes, I've told her. And what are you going to do with all that money, Jocelyne, do you have any idea?

That's just it, Papa, I don't know. What do you mean, you don't know? Anyone would know what to do with a sum like that. You could have a new life. But I like my life as it is, Papa. Do you think Jo would still love me as I am if he knew? Are you married? he asks. I lower my eyes. I don't want him to see my sadness. Do you have children, darling? Because if you do, spoil them; we never spoil our children enough. Do I spoil you, Jo?

Yes, Papa, every day. Oh, that's good. You make Maman and me laugh; even when you cheat at Monopoly and swear it isn't you cheating, that 500 note was there all the time among your pile of fives.

Maman is happy with you. Every evening when you come home, as soon as she hears your key in the lock, she has a charming way of tucking a stray lock of hair behind her ear and looking at herself furtively in the mirror. She wants to be pretty for you. She wants to be your present, your Belle du Seigneur. Do you think your mother will be here soon? Because she was going to bring me my newspaper and some shaving foam. I've run out. She'll be here soon, Papa. Good, good. What did you say your name was?

Six bloody minutes. They don't last long.

At the weekend, Jo takes me to Le Touquet. I've lost more weight; he's worried. You're working too hard, he says. The shop, the blog, giving Mado moral support. You ought to rest.

He's booked a room in the medium-priced Hôtel de la Forêt. We arrive at about four o'clock.

On the motorway, seven Porsche Cayennes passed us, and I noticed the way he looked at them every time. His sparkling little dreams.

They shine more brightly than usual.

We refresh ourselves in the bathroom and then go down the Rue Saint-Jean to the beach. He buys me some chocolates at the Chat Bleu. You're crazy, I whisper in his ear. You need to build your strength up, he says, smiling. There's magnesium in chocolate – it's good for stress. What surprising things you know, Jo.

Outside again, he takes my hand. You're a wonderful husband, Jo, I think; a big brother, a father, you're all the men a woman could need.

And maybe even an enemy, too. That's what I'm afraid of.

We walk on the beach for a long time.

Sand yachts speed past close to us, their sails snapping in the wind, making me jump every time, like the clusters of swallows flying low over Grandmother's house during my childhood summers. Out of season, Le Touquet looks like a picture postcard. Retired people, Labradors, people riding horses, and sometimes a few young women walking on the promenade with baby buggies. Out of season, Le Touquet is a place outside time. The wind whips at our faces, the salty air dries our skin; we shiver, we are at peace.

If he knew, just think of the fuss, it would be war. If he knew, wouldn't he want islands in the sun, tangy cocktails, burning sand? A huge bedroom, fresh sheets, glasses of champagne?

We walk for another hour and then go back to our hotel. Jo stops at the little bar and orders a non-alcoholic beer. I go upstairs to have a bath.

I look at my naked body in the bathroom mirror. My spare tyre has deflated, my thighs look slimmer. I have a body in transit between two weights. A soft, blurred body. But all the same, I like the look of it. It's touching. It suggests a blossoming to come. A new fragility.

I tell myself that if I were very rich, I'd think it ugly. I'd want a complete makeover. Breast implants. Liposuction. A tummy tuck. Cosmetic surgery, including an arm lift. And perhaps a little work on my eyelids.

Being rich means seeing all that's ugly and having the arrogance to think you can change things. All you have to do is pay for it.

But I'm not as rich as all that. I just happen to have a cheque for eighteen million five hundred and forty-seven thousand, three hundred and one euros and twenty-eight centimes, folded eight times and hidden inside a shoe. All I have is the temptation. A possible new life. A new house. A new TV set. Lots of new things.

But nothing really different.

Later, I rejoin my husband in the hotel restaurant. He has ordered a bottle of wine. We drink to each other. Let's hope nothing changes and we go on as we are, he says. *Nothing really different.*

Thank you, whoever's up there, for keeping me from cashing that cheque yet.

My wish list.

*A holiday alone with Jo (and not at the Sourire
    campsite. Tuscany?).*

Insist on a different room for Papa.

*Take Romain and Nadine to see Maman's grave.
    (Talk to them about her. And her currant loaf,
    yum yum.)*

Get my hair cut.

Sexy red lingerie. (It will drive you mad, Jo!)

That coat at Caroll's before someone else snaps

it up. QUICK!!

Have the sitting room redecorated. (Flat-screen TV???)

Change the garage door for an automatic one.

Have lunch at Taillevent in Paris some day. (Read a mouth-watering article in Elle à Table.*)*

Foie gras on gingerbread with the twins and fine wine, while we talk about men all through the night.

Ask Jo to make a shelter for the bins in the yard. (I hate recycling!!!)

Go back to Étretat.

Spend a week in London with Nadine. (Share her life. Love and cuddles. Read her The Little Prince. *My God, I must be crazy!)*

Pluck up the courage to tell Romain that I thought the girlfriend he brought home at Christmas was nasty, vulgar and, well, super-nasty. (Send him some money.)

Spend time at a spa. (Massage. Esthederm skin-care products? Simone Mahler?) Take care of myself. Oh, go away, there's nobody at home!

Eat better.

Go on a diet. (Both of the above.)

Dance with Jo to 'Indian Summer' on the next
    fourteenth of July.

Buy all the James Bond films on DVD. (???)

Ask the journalist to lunch. (Give her mother a
    present.)

A Chanel bag.

Louboutins.

Hermès. (Get them to unfold lots of scarves and
    then say, hm, I'll think it over.)

Buy a Seiko watch.

Tell everyone I was the winner of the eighteen
    million jackpot. (Eighteen million five hun-
    dred and forty-seven thousand, three hundred
    and one euros and twenty-eight centimes, to
    be precise.)

Be envied. At last!

Go to the Porsche showroom (in Lille? Amiens?).
    Ask for brochures about the Cayenne.

Go to a Johnny Hallyday concert at least once.
    Before he dies.

A Peugeot 308 with a satnav. (???)

To be told I'm beautiful.

I almost had a lover once.

It was not long after the birth of Nadège's dead body. When Jo was breaking things around the house and had stopped drinking eight or nine beers in the evening, slumped in front of the Radiola.

That was when he turned nasty.

Drunk, he just thought he was a big vegetable. A wimp; everything a woman hates in a man: vulgarity, egotism, thoughtlessness. But he stayed calm. A wimp, set in his ways, in fact congealed in them.

No, it was sobriety that turned Jo cruel. At first I put it down to coming off the booze. He'd replaced up to a dozen full-strength beers an evening by twice the number of low-alcohol Tourtels. You might have thought he wanted to drink them all to get at the 1% of alcohol each is supposed to contain, according to the tiny wording on the label, and be back in his inebriated comfort zone. But there was nothing at the bottom of those bottles, or himself, except sheer nastiness. The hateful things he said: it was your big body that suffocated Nadège. Every time you sat down you were strangling her. My baby's dead because you didn't take care of yourself. Poor Jo, your body is a dustbin, a great fat disgusting dustbin. You're a sow. A slag and a sow.

I took it all.

I didn't reply. I told myself that he must be suffering horribly. That the death of our little girl was sending him mad, and he was turning that madness on me. It was a black year, everything about it was dark. I used to get up in the night to go and cry in Nadine's room as she slept with her fists closed. I didn't want him to hear me and see how much he was hurting me. I didn't want the shame of that. I thought again and again of running away with the children, and then I told myself all this would pass. His grief would lift in the end, would simply leave us and go away. Some kinds of misery weigh so heavily that you have to let them go. You can't keep everything inside you. I stretched out my arms in the dark; I opened them hoping that Maman would walk into them. I prayed to feel her warmth around me; I didn't want the darkness to carry me away. But women are always alone in the face of men's ill-will.

If I didn't die then, it was first because of an ordinary little remark. Then because of the voice that spoke it. And then because of the mouth that voice came out of, and then the attractive face in which that mouth was smiling.

Let me help you.
Nice, 1994.

Eight months after we had buried Nadège. A horrible glossy white coffin. Two granite doves taking flight on her tombstone. I vomited; I couldn't bear it. Dr Caron, our present doctor's father, prescribed something for me. And then rest, and then good fresh air.

It was June. Jo and the children stayed in Arras. The factory, the end of the school year; their evenings without me; warming up meals in the microwave, watching videos, the moronic films you can indulge in when Maman is away; evenings telling yourselves she'll soon be back, things will get better. A little period of mourning.

I told the older Dr Caron that I couldn't cope with Jo's cruelty. I said things I never ought to have said. About my weaknesses, my feminine fears. I told him about my terror. I was ashamed, frozen, petrified. I wept, slobbered, held in his bony old arms, his pincers.

I wept over my husband's disgust. I had punished my murderous body; the point of the carving knife had drawn screams on my forearms; I had smeared my face with my guilty blood. I had gone mad. Jo's savagery had eaten me up, destroyed my strength. I could have cut out my tongue to silence him; I could have burst my eardrums so that I wouldn't hear him any more.

So when the older Dr Caron said, in a cloud of bad breath, 'I'm sending you away for a cure all by yourself for three weeks. I'm going to save you, Jocelyne,' his bad breath brought a ray of light.

And I went.

Nice, the Centre Sainte-Geneviève. The Dominican nuns were lovely. To see their smiles, you'd have thought there was no human atrocity that they couldn't imagine and yet still forgive. Their faces were luminous, like the faces of the saints on the little bookmarks in our childhood missals.

I shared a room with a woman the same age as Maman would have been now. As patients, she and I were both what the sisters called *mild* cases. We needed rest. We needed to find our way back to ourselves. Rediscover ourselves. Be reconciled to ourselves, in fact. Our status as *mild* cases meant we were allowed out.

Every afternoon, after the siesta, I walked down to the beach.

An uncomfortable beach, covered with pebbles. But for the sea, you'd have thought it a small stretch of wasteland. At the time of day when I go down there the sun is on your back as you look at the water. I'm putting on suncream. My arms are too short.

Let me help you.

My heart leaps. I turn round.

He's sitting two metres away from me, wearing a white shirt and beige trousers. His feet are bare. I can't see his eyes because of his dark glasses. I see his mouth. His lips – the lips coloured like a fruit that have just uttered those four audacious words. They are smiling. Then the atavistic prudence of all my female forebears resurfaces.

No, that wouldn't do.

Why wouldn't it do? Would it be wrong of me to want to help you, or for you to agree?

My God, I'm blushing. I snatch up my blouse to cover my shoulders.

I'm just leaving, anyway.

So am I, he says.

We don't move. My heart is racing. He's handsome, and I'm not pretty. He's a predator. A Lothario. A bad character, I'm sure of it. People don't speak to you like that in Arras. No man ventures to talk to you without first asking whether you're married. Or in a relationship with someone. Not this man. He comes in without knocking. Just shoulders his way in. A foot in the door. And I like it. I get to my feet. He's already standing up. He offers me his arm. I take it. My fingers feel the warmth of his tanned skin. Salt has left white marks on it. We leave the beach. We walk along the Promenade des Anglais with barely a metre between us. Further on, when we are opposite the Hôtel Negresco, his hand takes my elbow; he helps me across the road as if I were blind. I like the sense of vertigo. I close my eyes for a little while; I do as he wants. We go into the hotel. My heart is racing. I'm losing my mind. What has come over me? Am I going to go to bed with a stranger? I'm crazy.

But his smile reassures me. And then his voice.

Come on, I'll get you a cup of tea.

He orders two orange pekoes.

It's a light-bodied Ceylon tea, a pleasant

afternoon drink. Have you ever been to Ceylon
. . . Sri Lanka?

I laugh. I lower my eyes. I'm fifteen years
old, a romantic schoolgirl.

It's an island in the Indian Ocean less than
fifty kilometres from India. It became Sri Lanka
in 1972, when—

I interrupt him. Why are you doing this?

He delicately puts his cup of orange pekoe
down, and then takes my face in his hands.

I saw you on the beach from behind just
now, and I was overwhelmed by the loneliness
of your whole body.

He's good-looking. Like Vittorio Gassman in
Scent of a Woman.

I raise my face to his, my lips seek his, find
them. It's a strange, unexpected kiss; a kiss
warm with the flavour of the Indian Ocean. It's
a kiss that goes on a long time, a kiss that says
everything about what I lack, what he wants, my
sufferings, his impatience.

Our kiss is my rapture; my vengeance; all
the kisses I never had, from Fabien Derôme

in my class in middle school, from my timid 'Indian Summer' dance partner, from Philippe de Gouverne whom I never dared approach, from Solal, Prince Charming, Johnny Depp, Kevin Costner before the implants, all the kisses that girls dream of; the kisses before Jocelyn Guerbette's.

I gently push my stranger away.

I murmur: No.

He doesn't insist.

If he can read my mind just by looking at my back, now he can see in my eyes how afraid of myself I am.

I'm a faithful wife. Jo's cruelty isn't a good enough reason. My loneliness isn't a good enough reason.

I went home to Arras the next day. Jo's anger had died down. The children had made toasted ham and cheese sandwiches, and were praising the merits of *The Sound of Music*.

But nothing's ever as simple as that.

Since that article was published in *L'Observateur de l'Arrageois,* the world's gone mad.

The shop is never empty. The *tengoldfingers* blog gets eleven thousand hits a day. Our mini-merchandising site receives over forty orders daily. I'm sent thirty CVs a week. The telephone never stops ringing. People ask me to hold sewing workshops in schools. Embroidery workshops in hospitals. A hospice asks me to give knitting lessons, simple things like scarves and socks. The children's oncology department of the local hospital wants caps in cheerful colours. And sometimes gloves with two or three fingers. Mado is run off her feet, she's taking Prosoft, and when I worry she replies, with a nervous laugh twisting her mouth: If I stop, Jo, I shall fall down, and if I fall down I'll bring the whole place down with me, so don't stop me, keep pushing me, Jo, please keep pushing me. She's promised to go and see Dr Caron, to eat more salmon, to hang on. In the evening Jo gets me to recite the rules of nutritional safety and the principle of the cold chain, which he has to know for his exam to be a foreman. *'Deep-frozen foods' have undergone the process known as 'deep-freezing' in which the maximum crystallisation zone is passed as quickly as necessary, the effect being that the temperature of the produce is maintained (after thermal stabilisation) uninterruptedly at values below or equal to -18°C. Deep-freezing must be carried out without delay on produce of healthy and marketable quality using appropriate technical equipment. Only air, nitrogen and carbonic anhydride respecting the specific criteria of purity are authorised as refrigerant fluids.*

He's a sweet pupil who never loses his temper, except with himself. I encourage him. You'll make your dreams come true some day, dear Jo, I tell him, and then he takes my hand, carries it to his lips and says: It will be thanks to you, Jo, all thanks to you, and that makes me blush.

My God, if you knew. If you knew, what would become of you?

The twins have asked me to make waxed laces into little bracelets for them to sell in their salon. Every time someone has a manicure we manage to sell some little thing, says Françoise. So after that piece in *L'Observateur*, bracelets from your place will sell like hot cakes, adds Danièle. I make twenty. They're all sold by that evening. With the kind of luck you have, say the twins, you really ought to play the lottery. I laugh with them. But I'm afraid.

I've invited them to our house for dinner today.

Jo is charming and funny and helpful all evening. The twins have brought two bottles of

Veuve Clicquot. The bubbles in the wine, bursting on our palates, loosen our tongues. We are all mildly tipsy. And when you're tipsy your hopes and fears always rise to the surface.

We're nearly forty, says Danièle, if we don't meet a nice guy this year we're all washed up. Two nice guys, Françoise specifies. We laugh. But it's not funny. Maybe we're fated to stick together, like Siamese twins. Have you tried online dating? asks Jo. You bet. All we met were the weirdos. As soon as they find out we're twins, they just want a threesome. The thought of twins gets the guys excited, they suddenly think they've got two pricks. How about trying separately? suggests Jo. We'd rather die, they cry in chorus, before falling into each other's arms.

Glasses are topped up and emptied.

One day we'll have a big win, and we'll tell all those poor guys to piss off. We'll treat ourselves to gigolos, use them just once like Kleenex, then off they go! Into the bin! Next! They roar with laughter. Jo is looking at me;

he smiles. His eyes are shining. Under the table my foot has just found his.

I'm going to miss Jo.

He's off tomorrow for a week at the HQ of the Nestlé Group at Vevey in Switzerland, to finish his foreman's training and become a unit manager at Häagen-Dazs.

When he gets back we're going for a week-end at Cap Gris-Nez to celebrate. We've promised ourselves oysters and a big platter of *fruits de mer*. He's reserved a big room at Waringzelle Farm, only five hundred metres from the sea, where we can watch thousands of birds taking off for warmer countries. I'm proud of him. He'll be earning three thousand euros a month, and from then on he'll be part of the bonus system and have an insurance deal with a better company.

My Jo is getting closer to his dreams. We're getting closer to the truth.

How about you, Jocelyn? Danièle suddenly asks my husband, her voice slightly slurred because of the wine. Haven't you ever fantasised about having two women at once? Laughter. I pretend to take offence for the principle of the thing. Jo puts down his glass. With Jo, he replies, I have everything I need. She's sometimes so greedy that it's as if she *is* two women at once. More roars of laughter. I tap him smartly on the arm. Don't you listen to him! He'd say anything.

But the conversation is out of control, and reminds me of the discussions we have in summer, under the shade of the pine trees at the Sourire campsite, with JJ and Marielle Roussel and Michèle Henrion, when the heat and the pastis combined make us lose our heads and talk frankly about our regrets, our fears and what we lack. I must have the best collection of dildoes in the world, said Michèle Henrion with a sad smile last summer. At least they don't leave you after fucking you. And they don't go limp, added Jo, drunk as he was.

In time, as all women know, desire is amputated from sexuality. So we try to revive it, we offer it provocation in the shape of audacity, new experiences. In the months after my return from the Centre Sainte-Geneviève in Nice, our desire evaporated. Jo replaced it with brutality. He liked to take me quickly, from behind, hurting me. I hated that, bit my lips till the blood came so as not to scream with pain, but Jo was listening only to his own pleasure, and once he had ejaculated he quickly came out of me, put his trousers on and disappeared into the house or the garden with a non-alcoholic beer.

The twins are drunk when they leave, and Françoise has laughed so much that she has even wet herself slightly. Jo and I are left alone. The kitchen and dining room look like a battlefield. It's late. I'll clear up, you go to bed, I say. You have to leave early tomorrow morning.

Then he comes over to me and suddenly takes me in his arms and holds me close. Close to his own strength. His voice is soft, whispering in my ear. Thank you, dear Jo, he whispers. Thank you for everything you've done.

I turn pink; luckily he can't see that. I'm proud of you, I say. Go on, go to bed or you'll be tired tomorrow. The assistant manager of the factory is coming to pick him up at four-thirty in the morning. I'll make you a thermos flask of coffee.

Then he looks at me. There's a touch of sadness in his eyes. His lips are placed on mine, they open gently, his tongue slides worm-like into my mouth. It's a strangely sweet kiss, like a first kiss.

Or a last one.

L ist of crazy notions (with eighteen million in the bank).

Close the haberdashery shop and go back to studying fashion.
Get a Porsche Cayenne.
A house beside the sea. NO.
An apartment in London for Nadine.
A 34C bra, I've lost weight. NO NO NO. Are you crazy or what? Well, like I said, this is a list of my crazy notions. ☺

Lots of stuff from the Chanel boutique. NO.
A full-time nurse for Papa. (To have a new
    conversation with him every six minutes!!!)
Put some money aside somewhere safe for
    Romain. (He looks like he'll end up badly.)

Jo left two days ago.

I've gone to visit Papa. I tell him about my eighteen million again, the cross I have to bear. He can't believe his ears. He congratulates me. And what are you going to do with all that money, darling? I don't know, Papa. I'm scared. How about your mother? What does she think? I haven't told her yet, Papa. Come over here, my little girl, and tell me all your news. Jo and I are happy, I say, my voice unsteady. We've had our ups and downs like all couples, but we've managed to get over the bad times. We have two lovely children, a pretty little house, friends, we go on holiday twice a year. The shop is doing very well. The Internet site is developing, we already have eight people working on it. In a week's time Jo will be made foreman and put in charge of a production unit at the factory, and he's going to buy a flat-screen TV for the sitting room and ask for a loan to buy the car of his dreams. It's all rather fragile, but it holds together, I'm happy. I'm proud of you, murmurs my father, taking my hand in his. But about that money, Papa, I'm afraid it may . . . Who are you? he suddenly asks.

Bloody six minutes.

I'm your daughter, Papa. I miss you. I miss your cuddles. I miss the sound of the shower when you used to come home. I miss Maman. I miss my childhood. Who are you?

I'm your daughter, Papa. I have a haberdashery shop, I sell trouser buttons and zip fasteners because you were ill and I had to look after you. Because Maman died on the pavement when we were going shopping. Because I haven't had any luck. Because I wanted to kiss Fabien Derôme and it was that geek Marc-Jean Robert with his sketches on squared exercise-book paper, designed to score with the girls, who had my first kiss.

Who are you?

I'm your daughter, Papa. I'm your only daughter. Your only child. I grew up waiting for you and watching Maman draw the world. I grew up with the fear of not being pretty in your eyes, not lovely like Maman and brilliant like you. I dreamed of designing and creating dresses to make all women pretty. I dreamed of Solal, of a white knight, I dreamed of a perfect love story; I dreamed of innocence, of paradises lost, of lagoons; I dreamed that I had wings; I dreamed of being loved for myself without having to be kind and nice.

Who are you?

I'm the cleaning lady, monsieur. I've come to see if everything's all right in your room. I've come to clean your bathroom, the same as every day, empty the rubbish bin, put in a new plastic bag and clean up after you.

Thank you, mademoiselle, how charming you are.

At home, I reread the list of what I need, and it strikes me that wealth means being able to buy everything on it all at once, from the potato peeler to the flat-screen TV, by way of the coat from Caroll's and the non-slip mat for the bath. Go home with everything on the list, destroy the list and tell myself: Right, there we are, there's nothing else I need. All I have left from now on are wishes. Only wishes.

But that never happens.

Because our needs are our little daily dreams.

The little things to be done that project us into tomorrow, the day after tomorrow, the future; trivial things that we plan to buy next week, allowing us to think that next week we'll still be alive.

It's the need for a non-slip bath mat that keeps us going. Or for a couscous steamer. A potato peeler. So we stagger our purchases. We programme the places where we'll go for them. Sometimes we draw comparisons. A Calor iron versus a Rowenta iron. We fill our cupboards slowly, our drawers one by one. You can spend your life filling a house, and when it's full you break things so that you can replace them and have something to do the next day. You can even go so far as to break up a relationship in order to project yourself into another story, another future, another house.

Another life to fill.

I went into Brunet's bookshop in the Rue Gambetta and bought *Belle du Seigneur* in the Folio edition. I'm taking advantage of the evenings while Jo is away to reread it. But this time it's terrifying because now I know what happens. Ariane Deume takes a bath, soliloquises, gets ready, and I already know how the story will end in Geneva. I know about the dreadful triumph of boredom over desire, flushing passion away, but I still can't help believing in it. Weariness carries me off into the heart of the night. I wake up exhausted, dreamy, in love.

Until this morning.

When everything falls apart.

I didn't scream.

Didn't cry. Didn't lash out at the walls. Or tear my hair. Or break everything within reach. I didn't pass out. I didn't even feel my heart racing or a dizziness creeping over me.

All the same, I stayed sitting on the bed, just in case.

I looked around me. At our bedroom.

The little gilt frames with photos of the children at all ages. Our wedding photograph on Jo's bedside table. A portrait of me by Maman on my side of the bed; she painted it in a few seconds, starting with a violet swirl and using the blue watercolour she had left on her brush. That's you reading, she said.

My heart stayed steady. My hands didn't shake.

I bent down to pick up the blouse that I'd dropped on the floor. I put it on the bed beside me, and my fingers creased it before letting it fall. I'd iron it again in a moment. I ought to have listened to my inner prompting to buy the Calor steam turbo iron that I saw in Auchan at three hundred and ninety-nine euros, number twenty-seven on the list of things I need.

That was when I began to laugh. Laughing at myself.

I'd known it.

The plaster dust on the heel of my shoe confirmed it even before I looked.

Jo had repaired the hanging rail in the wardrobe, but more importantly, he had fixed the wardrobe itself to the wall, because it often looked as if it was about to fall over. So he had made two large holes in the back of the wardrobe and in the wall, which explained the plaster dust inside the wardrobe itself and on my shoes.

Once he had fixed the wardrobe to the wall, he must have wanted to wipe the floury dust off my shoes, and that's how he found the cheque.

When?

When had he found it? How long had he known?

As long ago as when I came home from Paris and he went to meet me at the station? When he murmured in my ear that he was glad to see me back?

Was it before Le Touquet? Had he taken me there knowing the harm he was going to do me? Did he take my hand on the beach already knowing that he was about to deceive me? And when we clinked glasses together in the hotel restaurant, and he vowed that nothing would change and it would all stay the same, did he already not give a shit? Was he preparing to make his getaway from our life?

Or was it after that, when we came home?

I don't remember when it was that he worked on the wardrobe. I wasn't there, and he hadn't said anything. The bastard. The thief.

Of course I called the Nestlé headquarters in Vevey.

They didn't know a thing about any Jocelyn Guerbette there.

The receptionist split her sides when I persisted, telling her that he was spending all week with them, training to be a foreman in charge of a unit at their Häagen-Dazs factory in Arras, yes, yes, Arras, mademoiselle, in France, in the Pas-de-Calais, postcode 62000. He was telling you the first thing that came into his head, dear. This is the headquarters of Nestlé Worldwide, you think we train foremen or stock controllers here? Oh, come off it! Tell the police if you like, or ask yourself if he has a mistress, but believe me, madame, he's not here. She must have realised that I was close to panic, because her voice suddenly became gentler, and before hanging up she added, I'm so sorry.

At the factory, Jo's boss confirmed my fears.

He had applied for a week's holiday and hadn't been in for the last four days. He's due back next Monday, I was told.

You don't say! You won't be seeing Jo again. No one will see the bastard again. He's made off with eighteen million in his pocket. The bird has flown. He'll have scratched the final *e* off my first name, and the cheque was suddenly made out in his name. Jocelyne minus her *e*. Jocelyn Guerbette. Four days will have given him enough time to get to the furthest reaches of Brazil. Canada. Africa. Switzerland, maybe. Eighteen million euros put a lot of distance between you and what you're leaving behind.

A hell of a lot of distance. A distance that can't be crossed.

The memory of our kiss five days ago. I knew it. It was a last kiss. Women always have presentiments about such things. It's our gift. But I hadn't listened to myself. I'd been playing with fire. I'd wanted to think that Jo and I would last forever. I'd let his tongue caress mine so incredibly gently, without daring to let my fear speak that evening.

I'd thought that after surviving the unbearable sadness of our little daughter's death, after the bad beers, the insults, the ferocity and the wounds it left, the brutal, animal sex, we had become inseparable, united, friends.

That was why the money had frightened me.

That was why I'd kept the astonishing win quiet. Why I'd controlled my hysteria. That was why, at heart, I hadn't wanted it. I'd thought that if I gave him his Cayenne he'd go off in it, drive a long way away, fast, never come back. Making other people's dreams come true means that you risk destroying them. He had to buy his car himself. For the sake of his pride. His wretched masculine pride.

I was right. I'd had a foreboding that the money would threaten us both. That it was fire. Incandescent chaos.

I knew in my bones that while it could do good, the money could also do harm.

Daisy Duck was right. *Greed burns everything in its path.*

I thought my love was a rampart. A dam that nothing could breach. I hadn't dared to imagine that Jo, my Jo, would rob me. Deceive me. Abandon me.

That he would destroy my life.

For, in the end, what was my life?

A happy childhood – until the middle of my seventeenth year, until Maman cried out in the street, and then a year later came Papa's stroke and his childlike wonder all over again every six minutes.

Hundreds of drawings and paintings recording those wonderful days: the long drive in the Citroën DS to the châteaux of the Loire, Chambord where I fell into the water and Papa and some other men jumped in to save me. More drawings: self-portraits of Maman in which she looks pretty, no suffering ever seems to show in her eyes. And a painting of the big house where I was born in Valenciennes, but I don't remember it myself.

My schooldays, simple and sweet. Even Fabien Derôme's non-kiss was a blessing, really. It taught me that ugly girls dream of handsome men, but all the pretty girls in the world stand between them and what they want, like so many peaks that can't be scaled. So from then on I had tried to see beauty where it might be hidden: in kindness, honesty, delicacy, and that was Jo. Jo and his forceful tenderness; he won my heart, married my body and made me his wife. I was always faithful to Jo, even in days of torment, on tempestuous nights. I loved him in spite of himself, in spite of the malice that disfigured his face and made him say such terrible things when Nadège died on the point of being born; as if, putting her nose out, she had sniffed the air, tasted the world and decided that she didn't like it.

My two live children and our little angel were my joy and my sorrow; I still tremble for Romain, but I know that on the day he is hurt and there's no one else to tend his wounds, he'll come back here. To my arms.

I loved my life. I loved the life that Jo and I had made. I loved the way that ordinary things became beautiful in our eyes. I loved our simple, comfortable, friendly house. I loved our garden, our modest little vegetable plot, the pathetic tomatoes on the vine it gave us. I loved hoeing the frozen ground with my husband. I loved our dreams of next spring. I was waiting with all the enthusiasm of a young mother to be a grandmother some day; I tried my hand at lavish cakes, gourmet pancakes, rich chocolate desserts. I wanted to have the scents of my own childhood in our house, with different photographs on the wall.

One day I was planning to convert a ground-floor room for Papa, I would have looked after him, and every six minutes I'd have invented a new life for him.

I loved my thousands of Isoldes who read *ten-goldfingers*. I loved their kindness, calm and powerful like a river flowing along, a regenerating force like a mother's love. I loved that community of women, our vulnerabilities, our strengths.

I loved my life deeply, but the moment that I won the lottery I knew that the money would wreck it all, and for what?

For a bigger vegetable plot? Larger, redder tomatoes? A new variety of tangerine? A larger, more luxurious house; a whirlpool bath? A Porsche Cayenne? A round-the-world cruise? A gold watch, diamonds? Enhanced breasts? A nose job? No, no and no again. I already had what money can't buy but can only destroy.

Happiness.

My happiness, anyway. Mine. With all its flaws, its banalities, its petty drawbacks. But mine.

A huge, flaming, unique happiness.

So I had made my decision a few days after coming back from Paris with the cheque: I had decided to burn the money.

But the man that I loved stole it.

I didn't say anything to anyone.

When the twins asked me about Jo, I said that he had stayed on in Switzerland for a few more days, at Nestlé's request.

Nadine was still sending me her news. She had a boyfriend, a tall redhead, a 3D film animator who was working on the next *Wallace and Gromit*. She was gently falling in love, my little girl; she didn't want to hurry things, she wrote in her latest email, because if you love someone and then you lose him you have nothing left. At last she was finding words. Tears came to my eyes. I wrote back saying that everything here was fine, I was going to sell the haberdashery shop (true) and devote myself to the website (false). I didn't say anything about her father. Or the harm he was doing us all. I promised to come and see her soon.

Romain, as usual, wasn't sending any news. I knew that he had left the Uriage crêperie and the girlfriend, and was now working in a video club in Sassenage. Probably with another girlfriend. He's a boy, said Mado. Boys are savages. And tears came to her own eyes, because she was reminded of her grown-up daughter who had died.

A week after the disappearance of Jo and my cheque for eighteen million euros, I gave a little party at the shop. There were so many people that they spilled out on to the pavement. I announced that I was leaving the haberdashery shop, and introduced the lady who was taking over from me: Thérèse Ducrocq, the mother of the journalist on *L'Observateur de l'Arrageois*.

Thérèse was applauded when she explained that she wasn't actually replacing me, just looking after the shop until I came back. Jo and I, I told my worried customers, had decided to take a year off. Our children were grown-up now. There were trips we'd promised ourselves ever since we first met, countries to be visited, cities to be explored, and we'd decided that now was the time. People came up to me, said they were sorry Jo wasn't here. They asked which cities we were going to visit, what countries we planned to travel to, what the climate was like there, and went on to offer to make us a sweater, a pair of gloves, a poncho. You've spoilt us so much all this time, Jo, it's our turn now.

Next day I shut up the house. Left the keys with Mado. And the twins drove me to Orly.

Are you sure about what you're doing, Jo? Oh, yes. Yes a hundred times, a thousand times over. Yes, I'm sure I want to leave Arras, where Jo left me. Leave our house, our bed. I know I won't be able to stand either his absence or the lingering odours of his presence. Of his shaving foam, his aftershave, the faint smell of his sweat in the clothes he's put in the washing, and the stronger smell of it in the garage, where he liked making small pieces of furniture; his acrid smell in the sawdust, in the air.

The twins go with me as far as they're allowed. Their eyes are flooded with tears. I try to smile.

It's Françoise who guesses. Puts the unimaginable into words.

Jo's left you, is that it? He's gone off with a younger, prettier woman now that he's going to be head of a unit and drive around in a Cayenne?

My own tears start flowing. I don't know, Françoise. He's gone. I have to lie about it. I avoid the trap, I resist temptation. The breach in the breakwater of my love. Maybe something's happened to him? suggests Danièle in a soothing voice. Don't people ever get kidnapped in Switzerland? I read somewhere that what with the private banking and laundered money, it's a bit like Africa there these days. No, Danièle, he hasn't been kidnapped, he's kidnapped himself from me, he's extracted, amputated, removed himself from me. And you didn't see it coming, Jo? Not at all. Nothing whatsoever. Like in a bad film. Your man goes away for a week, you reread *Belle du Seigneur* while you wait for him to come back, give yourself a face-mask, a body scrub, you wax your legs, you massage yourself with essential oils so as you'll be beautiful and soft when he comes back, and all of a sudden you know he won't be back at all. But how do you know, Jo? Did he leave you a letter, or something? I have to go. No, that's the worst of it, not even a letter, just nothing, a bleak void, like being in space.

Françoise takes me in her arms. I whisper in her ear for a moment, entrusting her with my final wishes. Call us when you arrive, she whispers back when I've finished. Have a good rest, adds Danièle. And if you need us to come, we'll be there.

I go through security. I turn round.

They're still there, their hands waving like birds.

And then I go.

I haven't gone very far.

It's fine in Nice. It isn't the holiday season yet, just the in-between season. A season for convalescence. I go down to the beach every day at the time when the sun will shine on my back.

I have the figure that was mine before Nadine, the figure I had before I put on all the flesh that stifled Nadège. I'm pretty, I look the way I did when I was twenty.

Every day, even when the sun isn't strong,

I put suncream on my back, and my arms are still too short; and every day, at that precise moment, my heart races and my senses sharpen. I've learnt to hold myself upright, to move with assurance. To get rid of that look of solitude. I gently massage my shoulders, my neck, my shoulder blades – my fingers move over my skin, there's nothing tentative about them; I remember his voice. The words he said seven years ago, when I came here to escape the horrible things Jo had said.

Let me help you.

But the words behind my back today come from people chatting into their mobile phones, from kids who come here to smoke and laugh after school. The tired words of young mothers, already so lonely, their babies left in the shade in buggies, their husbands who have gone away, who don't touch them any more; their words are salty, like tears.

So, in the afternoon, when I've counted forty planes taking off, I pick up my things and go back to the studio flat that I've rented for a few weeks, time enough for me to learn how to be an assassin, in the Rue Auguste-Renoir, behind the Musée des Beaux-Arts Jules Chéret.

It's a nondescript flat in a 1950s apartment block, designed when the architects of the Côte d'Azur were dreaming of Miami, motels and buildings full of curves; the time when they dreamed of taking flight. It's furnished. The furniture is tasteless but it's solid, that's all you can say for it. The bed creaks, but as I sleep alone the creaking doesn't bother anyone but me. I can't see the sea from the only window, where I dry my underwear. In the evening the place smells of the wind, of salt and diesel. In the evening I dine alone, I watch TV alone and I am alone with my insomnia.

I still cry in the evenings.

As soon as I get back from the beach I shower, as Papa did when he came home. But I do it not to get rid of any residue of glutaraldehyde, only to wash away my shame, my pain. My lost illusions.

I'm preparing myself.

During those first weeks after Jo made off, I went back to the Centre Sainte-Geneviève. The Dominican nuns had gone away too, but the nurses who had replaced them were just as considerate.

When he left me, Jo took away my laughter, my joy, my love of life.

He tore up the list of my needs, my desires, the list of my crazy ideas.

He'd deprived me of the little things that keep us going. The potato peeler you plan to buy at Lidl tomorrow. The Calor iron you're going to buy at Auchan the week after that. A little rug for Nadine's room in a month's time, when the payslip comes in.

He'd taken away my desire to be beautiful, sexy, a good lover.

He had crossed out my memories of us, cancelled them. He'd done irreparable damage to the simple poetry of our life. A stroll, hand in hand, on the beach at Le Touquet. Our hysterical delight when Romain took his first steps. When Nadine first said *pipi*, wee-wee, when she meant Papa because she was pointing at him. A fit of laughter when we'd made love at the Sourire campsite. Our hearts racing at the same moment when Denny Duquette appears to Izzie Stevens again in season five of *Grey's Anatomy*.

When he left me because he'd robbed me, Jo wrecked everything he'd left behind him. Soiled it all. I had loved him, and now I had nothing left.

The nurses gently taught me to regain my taste for certain things. The way you teach famine-stricken children to eat again. The way you learn to live again at the age of seventeen when your dead mother wets herself on the pavement in full view of everyone. The way you learn to think yourself pretty again, to tell yourself lies and forgive yourself. They erased my black thoughts, brought light into my night-mares. They taught me to breathe from lower down in the body, from the stomach, well away from the heart. I wanted to die, I wanted to run away. I no longer wanted any of what my life had been. I had inspected the weapons available to me, and retained two of them.

Throwing myself under a train. Cutting my wrists.

Throwing myself off a railway bridge as a train was passing. You couldn't miss. Your body would explode, be torn to pieces, scattered over several kilometres. There wouldn't be any pain. Only the sound of your body falling through the air, and the terrifying screech of the train, then the *whoomph* of the former hitting the latter.

Cutting the veins in my wrists. Because there was something romantic about that. The bath, the candles, the wine. A kind of amorous ceremonial. Like the baths taken by Ariane Deume, preparing herself for her Seigneur. Because the pain of the blade on my wrist would be tiny, and aesthetically pleasing. Because the warm blood would spurt out, a comforting sight, drawing red flowers that would blossom in the water, tracing perfumed trails. Because it wouldn't really be like dying, more like going to sleep. My body would slip down, my face would sink and I would drown in dense, comfortable liquid red velvet; like a womb.

The nurses at the Centre taught me to kill only what had killed me.

So here we have our runaway.

He's shrunk, he's shrivelled up. His forehead is pressed to the window of the moving train, its speed creating virtuoso Impressionist pictures of the fields. He turns his back to the other passengers, like a child sulking, although his problem is not a fit of the sulks but treachery, a stab wound inflicted with a knife.

He had found the cheque. He had waited for her to tell him about it. He had taken her to Le Touquet for that; for nothing. Then, given her craving for calm, her love of things that last, he had guessed what Jocelyne had in mind. He had taken the money because she was going to burn it. Or give it away. To drooling sufferers from muscular dystrophy, bright little kids with cancer. It was more money than he could earn with Häagen-Dazs in six hundred years. Now he utters a sob as he feels his disgust at himself rising to terrifying fruition. The woman next to him asks in a whisper, 'Are you all right, monsieur?' He reassures her with a weary gesture. The train window is cold against his forehead. He remembers Jocelyne's cool, gentle hand when he was almost carried off by that bad attack of flu. Pretty images always come to the surface when you'd like to drown them.

When the train reaches Brussels Midi he waits for all the other passengers to get out before leaving the carriage himself. His eyes are red, like the eyes of men not properly awake, half closed to keep warm in the draughty bars of railway stations, men who dunk Belgian speculoos biscuits or rolls in their strong coffee. It is the first coffee of his new life, and it is not a good one.

He has chosen Belgium because they speak French there, and it is the only language he knows. Although he didn't know all the words in it, as he had told Jocelyne when he was courting her. She had laughed and tried the word *symbiosis* on him, and when he shook his head she had said it was what she expected of love, and their hearts had raced together.

He walks through the drizzling rain that stings his skin. See, he is making faces, he looks ugly. He was handsome when Jocelyne looked at him. He looked like Venantino Venantini. On some days he was the most handsome man in the world. He crosses the Boulevard du Midi, goes along the Boulevard de Waterloo, up the Avenue Louise and the Rue de la Régence to the Place du Grand Sablon and the house he has rented there. He wonders why he chose such a big one. Perhaps he believes he'll be forgiven. Perhaps he thinks that Jocelyne will come and join him there one day, that one day the things that can't be explained will be understood. That one day they will all be reunited, even angels and dead little girls. He thinks he ought to have looked up the definition of *symbiosis* in the dictionary at the time. But for the moment, excitement carries him away. He is a rich man. The world is his to command.

He buys a very powerful, very expensive red car, an Audi A6 RS. He buys a Patek Philippe watch that displays the date as well as the time, and an Omega Speedmaster Moonwatch. A Loewe flat-screen television set and the collector's edition of the Jason Bourne trilogy. He is catching up with his dreams. He buys a dozen Lacoste shirts. A pair of Berluti ankle boots. A pair of Weston shoes, a pair of Bikkembergs. He has a suit made to measure by Dormeuil. Another by Dior, but he doesn't like it. He throws it out. He gets a cleaning lady for the big house. He lunches in the cafés around the Grand-Place. El Greco, Le Paon. In the evening he sends out for a pizza or some sushi. He goes back to drinking real beer, the kind drunk by lost men with blurred vision. He likes Bornem Triple, loves the giddiness you get from Kasteelbier with its 11° alcohol content. His features are thickening. He is slowly putting on weight. He spends his afternoons on café terraces trying to make friends. Conversations are few and far between. People are alone with their mobiles, sending thousands of words out into the void of their lives. At the tourism office in the Rue Royale, they recommend a cruise for bachelors along the canals of Brussels, two women on it among twenty-one starving men; it's like a bad film. At the weekend he goes to the seaside. In Knokke-le-Zoute he stays at the Manoir du Dragon or the Rose de Chopin. He lends money and never sees it again. Sometimes he goes out in the evenings. He goes to nightclubs, exchanges a few dismal kisses, tries to seduce a few girls. They laugh at him. Things are not going very well. He pays for a lot of champagne and is sometimes allowed to touch a breast, a dry, purplish cunt. His nights are gloomy and cold and disenchanted. He goes home alone. He drinks alone. He laughs alone.

He watches films alone. Sometimes he thinks of Arras, and then he opens another beer to drive the thought away, to blur everything again.

And sometimes he picks a girl on the Internet, as you might choose a dessert from a restaurant trolley. The girl comes to give herself to him in the darkness of his big house, she swallows up his banknotes and hardly even has to suck him off because he can't get a hard-on. Look at him when she slams the door behind her: he slips to the cold, tiled floor, a pathetically sad figure, hunched up like an old dog; he sobs, he slobbers out his fears with the snot from his nose, and no kindly woman holds out her arms to him in the shadows of his night.

It is six months after Jocelyn Guerbette left Arras that the cold takes possession of him.

He has a hot shower, but the cold is still there. His skin gives off steam, but he is still shivering. The flesh of his fingers is blue and wrinkled, and seems about to peel away. He wants to go home. He is falling to pieces. Money doesn't buy you love. He misses Jocelyne. He thinks of her laugh, the smell of her skin. He loves their partnership, their two living children. He loves the fear he sometimes felt that she might become too beautiful, too intelligent for him. (And he loved the idea that he might lose her; it made him a better husband.) He loves it when she raises her eyes from a book to smile at him. He loves her steady hands, her forgotten dreams of being a dress designer. He loves her love and her warmth, and suddenly understands his present icy chill. Being loved warms the blood, heats desire. He emerges from the shower still trembling. He doesn't hit the wall as he was still doing not so long ago. He has succeeded in taming his sorrow for Nadège, he doesn't talk about it any more; he won't hurt Jocelyne like that again.

He doesn't open his bottle of beer. His lips are shaking. His mouth is dry. He looks at the big sitting room around him, the emptiness. He doesn't like that white sofa. That low, gilded table. The magazines that no one reads, arranged on it to look pretty. This evening he doesn't like the red Audi, the Patek watch, the girls you can buy who don't take you in their arms; his thickened body, his swollen fingers, and this icy chill.

He doesn't open the bottle of beer. He gets to his feet, leaves the light on in the hall, just in case Jocelyne were to track him down tonight, just in case leniency were to knock at the door, and he goes upstairs. It is a large staircase; images of falling surface in his mind. *Vertigo. Gone With the Wind. Battleship Potemkin*. Blood flowing out of your ears. Bones breaking.

His fingers clutch the banister; the idea of forgiveness comes only after you have picked yourself up.

He leaves for London. Two hours in the train; his hands are moist for those two hours. As if he were going on a first date. Forty metres under the sea, he is afraid. He is going to see Nadine. She refused at first. He persisted, he almost begged her. A matter of life and death. She thought that expression extremely melodramatic, but it made her smile, and he took advantage of that smile.

They are going to meet in the Caffè Florian, on the third floor of Harrods, the famous department store. He is early. He wants to be able to choose a good table, a good chair. He wants to see her arrive. Have time to recognise her. He knows that sorrow rearranges faces, changes eye colour. A waitress comes over. With a gesture, he lets her know that he doesn't want anything. He is ashamed of himself for not even being able to say, in English: I'm waiting for my daughter, I don't feel very well, mademoiselle, I'm frightened, I've done something very stupid.

There she is. She is beautiful and slender, and he sees Jocelyne's grace and touching pallor in Madame Pillard's haberdashery shop, back when he could never have imagined becoming a thief, a murderer. He gets up. She smiles. She's a woman now; how quickly time passes. His hands are shaking. He doesn't know what to do. But she holds her face up to his. Kisses him. Hello, Papa. *Papa*; that was a thousand years ago. He has to sit down, he's not feeling very well, he needs air. She asks if he is all right. He says,

Yes, yes, it's just the emotion, I'm so happy to see you. You're so beautiful.

He has dared to say that to his daughter. She doesn't blush, indeed, she is rather pale. She says, It's the first time in my life you've said anything like that to me, Papa, something so personal. She might cry, but she is strong. He is the one who cries, an old man. He is the one who appeals to her. Listen to him. You're so beautiful, my little girl, like your mother. Like your mother.

The waitress comes over again, gliding silently like a swan. Gently, Nadine says *Just a few minutes, please*, and Jocelyn realises from the music of his daughter's voice that he has only one chance to talk to her, and that chance is now. So he plunges in desperately. I stole from your mother. I betrayed her. I ran away. I'm ashamed, and I know that my shame comes too late. I . . . I . . . He is searching for words. I. The words won't come. This is difficult. Tell me how I can get her to forgive me. Help me.

Nadine raises her hand. It's over already. The

waitress is back. *Two large coffees, two pieces of fruit cake. Yes, madam.* The thief doesn't understand a word of it, but he likes the sound of his daughter's voice. They look at each other. Sorrow has changed the colour of Nadine's eyes. They used to be blue in Arras. They are grey now, a rainy grey; a street drying off. She looks at her father. She is searching for what her mother loved in that sad, flabby face. She is trying to discover the features of the Italian actor with his clear laughter and white teeth. She remembers the attractive face that used to kiss her goodnight when she went to bed in the evening; her father's kisses that tasted of ice cream – vanilla, cookies, praline, banana or caramel ice cream. Does what you experienced as beautiful turn ugly because the person who made your life better has let you down? I don't know how you can get her to forgive you, Papa, says Nadine. All I know is that Maman is unhappy; her whole world has crumbled.

And when she adds, five seconds later, so has mine, he knows that it's all over.

He puts out his hand to his daughter's face; he would like to touch it, caress it one last time, warm himself on it, but his hand is frozen. It is a strange, sad farewell. Finally Nadine lowers her eyes. He understands that she is letting him go without watching him, without the insult of watching a coward take to his heels. It is her present to him, in return for being told that she is beautiful.

In the train going back, he remembers what his own mother had said when she was told that her husband had just died of a heart attack at the office. He's abandoned me, your father has deserted us! The bastard, what a bastard! And later, after the funeral, when she was told that his heart had given out while he was having leisurely sex with the woman in charge of office equipment, a divorcée with a taste for good living, she had killed herself. That was it. She had taken the words back into herself, sealed her lips and Jocelyn, still a child, had seen the cancer of the evil that men implant in women's hearts.

Back in Brussels, he goes to the Tropismes

bookshop in the Galeries des Princes shopping arcade. He remembers the book from which she sometimes looked up to smile at him. She was beautiful when she was reading. She seemed happy. He asks for *Belle du Seigneur*, chooses the large-format edition, the one she used to read. He also buys a dictionary. Then he spends his days reading. He looks up the definitions of words he doesn't understand. He wants to find out what made her dream, what made her beautiful, what made her look up at him sometimes. Perhaps she saw him as Adrien Deume, and perhaps that was why she loved him. Men think they are lovable as lordly *seigneurs* like Solal, when they may just be frightening. He hears the sighs of Ariane, the *belle*; the private thoughts of the woman whose religion is love. The length of the monologues is sometimes tedious. He wonders why there isn't more punctuation for several pages; then he reads the text aloud, and in the echo of the large sitting room his breathing changes, speeds up; he suddenly feels dizzy, as one might in the midst of rapture; there is something feminine, gracious about it, and he understands Jocelyne's happiness.

But the final part of the book is cruel. In Marseille, Solal strikes Ariane and makes her sleep with her former lover; the *belle* behaves like a graceless prostitute. And then comes the ending in Geneva. As he closes it, Jocelyn wonders whether the book comforted his wife by making her think that she had gone beyond 'the boredom and lassitude' that consumed the romantic lovers, and that in her own way she had discovered a love of a perfection not to be found in expensive clothes, hats and hairstyles, but in trust and peace.

Perhaps *Belle du Seigneur* was a book about loss, but Jocelyne read it to assess what she had saved.

He wants to go back now. He has plenty of words for her, words he has never spoken before. He knows what *symbiosis* means.

He is afraid to telephone. He is afraid to hear her voice. He is afraid that she will not pick up the phone. He is afraid of silence and sobbing.

He wonders if he shouldn't just go back, arrive this evening at the peaceful dinner hour, put the key in the lock, open the door. Believe in miracles. Believe in Reggiani's song, with words by Dabadie. *Is there anybody there? / Anyone I can see? / I can hear the dog from here. / So if you are not dead / Open the door to me. / I know that I'm late home.* But suppose she has changed the locks? Suppose she isn't there? He decides to write a letter.

Later, weeks later, when he has finished the letter, he takes it to the post office in the Place Poelaert near the Palais de Justice. He is worried. He wonders, several times, if he has put enough postage on it. It is an important letter. He watches the hand throwing his letter full of hopes and new beginnings into the basket; other letters soon fall in with it, covering his, suffocating it, hiding it. He feels lost. He *is* lost.

He goes back to the big, empty house. There is nothing left in it but the white sofa. He has sold or given away everything else. The car, the TV set, *The Bourne Trilogy*, the Omega watch, he couldn't find the Patek, but he doesn't care.

He waits on the white sofa. He waits for a reply to slide under his door. He waits a long, long time, but no reply comes. He trembles, and over the following days, when nothing happens, his cold body goes numb. He no longer eats or moves. He drinks a few mouthfuls of water every day, and when all the bottles are empty he stops drinking anything. Sometimes he sheds tears. Sometimes he talks to himself. He says both their names. That was the symbiosis, only he didn't see it.

When his death throes begin, he is happy.

The sea is grey in Nice.

There's a heavy swell far out. Lacy crests of foam. A few sails moving in the wind, like hands calling for help, but no one can catch hold of them.

It is winter.

Most of the shutters in the apartment buildings on the Promenade des Anglais are down. They are like medical dressings on the well-worn façades. The old people are shut up at home, watching the news and the bad weather forecast on TV. They chew for a long time before swallowing. They are suddenly making things last. Then they go to sleep on the sofa with a little woolly rug over their knees and the TV still on. They must hold out until spring or they'll be found dead; with the rising temperature of the first fine days, disgusting smells will seep out from under doors, up chimneys, nightmarish. Their children are far away. They won't come back until the first warm days, when they can take advantage of the sea, the sun, Grandpa's apartment. They'll come back when they can take measurements, draw up plans: enlarge the sitting room, give the bedrooms and the bathroom a makeover, fit a new fireplace, put an olive tree in a pot on the balcony so that they can eat their own olives some day.

It's almost a year and a half ago that I was sitting here on my own, in the same place, at the same time of year. I was cold, and I was waiting.

I had just left the nurses at the Centre, alive, appeased. In those few weeks I had killed something in me.

A terrible thing called kindness.

I had drained myself of it like pus, like a dead baby; a present someone has given you only to take it back immediately.

An atrocity.

It's nearly eighteen months since I let myself die and be born again as someone else. Colder, more angular. Grief always refashions you in a strange form.

And then Jo's letter had arrived, a small highlight in the mourning of the woman I was then. An envelope sent from Belgium; on the back, a Brussels address in the Place du Grand Sablon. Inside, four pages of his untidy handwriting. Surprising phrases, new words that might have been taken straight from a book. *Jo, I know now that love can stand up to death better than to betrayal.*[*] His writing was full of fear. The gist of it was that he wanted to come back. Just like that. Back home. Back to our house. The factory. The garage. The small items of furniture that he

[*] Adapted from André Maurois (1815–1967), 'Love can stand up to absence or death better than to doubt or betrayal.'

made. Back to our laughter. And the Radiola TV set, the low-alcohol beer, his friends on a Saturday, my only real friends, he called them. *And you.* He wanted to come back and find me as I was. I want to be loved by you again, he wrote, I have realised that *to love is to understand*.[*] He promised. I'll persuade you to forgive me. I was afraid, I ran away. He swore. He made declarations. I love you, he wrote. I miss you. He was suffocating. I know that he wasn't lying, but it was too late for these careful, pretty words.

My merciful curves had melted away. The ice was taking shape, and it had a cutting edge to it.

He had enclosed a cheque with his letter.

Fifteen million one hundred and eighty-six thousand and four euros, seventy-two centimes.

Made out to Jocelyne Guerbette.

Look, I'm asking you to forgive me, said the figures. Forgive my betrayal, my cowardice; forgive my crime, my lack of love.

[*] After Françoise Sagan (1935–2004), 'To love is not just to love well but above all to understand.' (In Qui je suis.)

Three million three hundred and sixty-one thousand, two hundred and ninety-six euros, fifty-six centimes had vanquished his dream and his self-disgust.

I expect he bought his Porsche, his flat-screen TV, all the James Bond films, a Seiko watch, a Patek Philippe, maybe a Breitling, shiny and flashy, several women younger and more beautiful than me, depilated, Botoxed, perfect; he must have had some bad experiences, as people do when they have a treasure trove – remember the cat and the fox who steal the five gold pieces given to Pinocchio by Mangiafuoco? He must have lived like a prince for a while, as you always want to do when fortune suddenly comes your way, to get your revenge for not having it sooner, for not having had it at all. Five-star hotels, Taittinger Comtes de Champagne, caviar; and then whims and fancies, yes, I can easily imagine my thief developing them: I don't like this room, the shower drips, the meat is overdone, the sheets are scratchy; I want another girl; I want friends.

I want what I've lost.

I never replied to my murderer's letter. I let it slip out of my hands – the sheets fluttered for a moment, and when they finally came down they were reduced to ashes, and I began to laugh.

M y last list.

Go to the hairdresser, have a manicure and
    depilation (for the first time in my life get
    someone other than me to remove the hair
    from my legs / armpits / bikini line — well,
    not the full Brazilian, all the same).
Spend two weeks in London with Nadine and her
    red-headed lover.
Give her the money to make her next little film
    (she's sent me the screenplay, from a short

story by Saki, it's brilliant!!!)
Open a savings account for my rascal of a son.
Choose a new wardrobe (I'm a size 10 now!!!!
    Men smile at me in the street!!!!).
Organise an exhibition of Maman's drawings.
Buy a house with a big garden and a terrace
    with a view of the sea, maybe at Cap Ferrat,
    where Papa will be comfortable. Above all,
    don't ask the price, just write the cheque,
    casually ☺.
Get Maman's grave moved to near me and Papa.
    (In the garden of the house mentioned
    above?)
Give a million to someone at random. (Who?
    How?)
Live with him. (Well, beside him, really.) And
    wait ☺.
And that's all.

I did everything on my last list with the exception of a couple of details

In the end I did have a full Brazilian wax – it's odd, very little girl-like – and I haven't decided who to give the million to yet.

I'm waiting for an unexpected smile, a small ad in the newspaper, a sad but kindly look; I'm waiting for a sign.

I spent two wonderful weeks in London with my daughter. I found my way back to the old times, when Jo's cruelty made me take refuge in her room, and she stroked my hair until I was as calm as the surface of a lake again. She thought I looked pretty, I thought she looked happy. Her lover Fergus is the only Irishman in England who doesn't drink beer, and that made me a happy mother. One morning he took us to Bristol and showed me round the studio where he was working; he lent my face to a florist whom Gromit was passing as a tiny dog pursued him. It was a lovely day, like going back to childhood.

When we said goodbye at St Pancras, we didn't shed any tears. Nadine told me that her father had been to see her some time ago; he looked lost, she said, but I wasn't listening. Then she whispered maternal words in my ear: You deserve a good life, Maman. Try to be happy with him.

Him. My Vittorio Gassman; I've been living at his side for over a year and a half now. He's as good-looking as he was on the day when we kissed in the Hôtel Negresco, his lips still taste of orange pekoe tea, but when they kiss mine now my heart doesn't race, my skin doesn't shiver.

He was the only island in my sorrow.

I had called him just after Jo's foreman confirmed that he was taking a week's holiday. On the day when I knew I had been deceived. I had phoned, not for a moment believing that he would remember me; perhaps he was only a predator who duped faithful wives with a cup of tea at the bar of the Hôtel Negresco, with its delicious temptation of dozens of empty rooms. He knew who I was at once. I was hoping to hear from you, he said. His voice was grave and calm. He listened to me. He understood my anger and the mutilation I had suffered. And he said those four respectful words: *Let me help you.*

They were an open sesame. They lanced the boil. Made me the ethereal *Belle*, Ariane Deume on the edge of the void in Geneva, one Friday afternoon in September 1937.

I let him help me. I gave myself up to him.

We go down to the beach every day, and every day we sit on the uncomfortable pebbles.

I didn't want little canvas chairs or cushions. I want everything to be the way it was on our first day, the day when I dreamed of perhaps becoming his lover; the day when I decided that neither Jo's harsh words nor my loneliness was a good enough reason for that. I don't regret any of it. I gave myself to Jo. I loved him without reservation or afterthought. I have ended up treasuring the memory of his moist hand on mine during our first date at the newsagent's in the Arcades; I could still weep for joy when I close my eyes and hear those first words of his: *You're the miracle.* I'd accustomed myself to his acrid, animal body odour. I had forgiven him a great deal, because love calls for a great deal of forgiveness. I had been prepared to grow old with him although he never said pretty things to me, no flowery phrases – oh, you know, those silly things that win girls' hearts and make them remain faithful for ever.

I tried to lose weight, not so that he would think me more beautiful but so that he could be proud of me.

You're beautiful, says the man who is now reaping the benefit of it, although I wanted to be beautiful for someone else. But I would like to see you smile sometimes, Jo. He's a good man; he has never known betrayal. His love is patient.

I sometimes do smile in the evenings, when we go home to the huge, beautiful villa in Villefranche-sur-Mer that I bought, signing the sales agreement *casually* and the cheque *without a moment's thought*; when I see Papa sitting on the terrace with his nurse beside him, while Papa looks at the sea and, with his child's eyes, searches the clouds for images: bears, maps of a Promised Land, Maman's drawings.

I smile for six minutes as I invent a new life for him in the cool of the evening.

You're a famous doctor, Papa, you've done outstanding research; you were made Chevalier de la Légion d'Honneur at the prompting of Hubert Curien when he was Minister of Research. You perfected a treatment to counteract ruptured aneurisms. It's based on the enzyme 5-lipoxygenase, and you were on the shortlist for the Nobel Prize. You'd even written a speech in Swedish: you came to my room every evening to rehearse it, and I laughed at your guttural accent. But Sharp and Roberts won the prize that year for their discovery of split genes.

That was yesterday, and Papa had liked the sound of his life.

This evening: You're a fabulous countertenor. You're so handsome that you have the women shrieking and their hearts beating faster. You studied at the Schola Cantorum in Basle, and your performance in Handel's *Giulio Cesare in Egitto* made your name. Oh yes, and that was how you met Maman. She went to the dressing room to congratulate you after you sang from it in a recital, carrying a bouquet of thornless roses. She was crying. You fell in love with her, and she took you in her arms.

Tears of happiness rise to his shining eyes.

Tomorrow I'll tell you that you were the most wonderful of fathers. I'll remind you how Maman made you take a shower when you came home, because she was afraid that didecyl chloride would turn us all into monsters out of the comedy film *La Soupe aux Choux*. I'll tell you about our games of Monopoly, I'll tell you you used to cheat so that I could win, and I'll admit that you once told me I was beautiful, and I believed you, and it made me cry.

Yes, I do smile in the evening; sometimes.

The house is silent.

Papa is asleep in his cool ground-floor room. The nurse has gone to meet her fiancé, a tall young man with a nice smile who dreams of Africa, and of schools and wells there (a candidate for my million?).

We were drinking a tisane just now, my Vittorio Gassman and I, on the shady terrace; his hand was trembling in mine, I know that I'm not sure, it could be the wind, a branch moving, maybe; I'm so uneasy about men these days, I can't help it.

He rose in silence, dropping a kiss on my forehead. Don't be too late, Jo. I'll be waiting for you. And before he goes to our room, in the hope of a cure for me that won't come this evening, he puts on the CD of that Mozart aria I love so much, just loud enough for it to fill the terrace with sound but not to wake up the fabulous countertenor, the Monopoly cheat and the man who almost won the Nobel Prize.

And this evening, as they do every evening, my lips in perfect synchronisation echo those of Kiri Te Kanawa, articulating Countess Almaviva's moving aria: *Dove sono i bei momenti / Di dolcezza e di piacer? / Dove andaro i giuramenti / Di quel labbro menzogner? / Perché mai se in pianti e in pene / Per me tutto si cangio / La memoria di quel bene / Dal mio sen non trapasso?*

---

* Where are those beautiful moments / of tenderness and pleasure? / Where are the vows / of those lying lips? / Why has everything changed / into tears and pain for me? / Why has the memory / not left my heart?
(*The Marriage of Figaro, Act III*).

I sing for myself, in silence, my face turned to the dark sea.

I am loved. But I no longer love.

From: mariane62@yahoo.fr

To: Jo@tengoldfingers.com

Hello Jo. I've been a faithful reader of your blog from the start. It was a comfort at a time when things weren't going very well in my life, and I clung to your tacking thread and Azurite yarns so that I wouldn't fall . . . Thanks to you and your lovely words, I didn't. Thank you with all my heart. Now it's my turn to be there for you if you would like, if you need someone. I just wanted you to know. Mariane.

From: sylvie-poisson@laposte.net

To: Jo@tengoldfingers.com

I love your blog, but why aren't you writing it any more? Sylvie Poisson, from Jenlain.

PS I don't mean that what Mado and Thérèse are writing isn't good, but it's not the same thing J.

From: mariedorves@yahoo.fr

To: Jo@tengoldfingers.com

Hello Jo. Do you member me? You replide to me so nicely when I sent you good wishes for your husband with flu. You seemd so in love it would do anyone good. My husband died at work resently, a concrete making machine fell on his head on a building cite, and in your note that I read at the semetary you say we all have just one love and for me it was my Jeannot. I miss him and you too. No more now cause I'm gonna cry.

From: françoise-et-daniele@coiffesthetique_arras.fr

To: Jo@tengoldfingers.com

Jo, you're totally nuts! You're crazy!!! Crazy, crazier, craziest! They're wonderful. And with the Onion Jacques* painted on the roof and the chrome rear-view mirrors they're lovely, lovely, lovely like in Cloclo's song! They're the cutest Minis anyone ever saw. The people around here think it was us who won a big prize, imagine that! We have lots of guys chasing us now, we get sent flowers, poems, chocolates, we'll end

* Union Jack pronounced with a French accent

up as fat as a couple of pigs!!!! There's even a boy of fifteen who's in love with us both and wants to run away with us. He waits for us every evening behind the belfry with his suitcase, would you believe it? One evening we hid to see what he looks like, he's really cute!!! Fifteen years old, imagine that! And he wants us both, ha ha! In his last letter he said he was going to kill himself if we didn't turn up, talk about irresistible! The salon is full all the time, we had to take on two girls, one of them is Juliette Bocquet, you may remember her, she used to go out with Fabien Derôme and it ended badly because her parents thought he'd made her pregnant, oh well, that's all in the past. With your Minis we're the belles of Arras now, and soon we'll come down and see you even if you say no, it will be a surprise! Well, we suppose you know what happened to Jo, how the neighbours called the police because of the smell; it was a shock for everyone here, particularly because he was smiling, but we don't talk about it any more.

Nearly two already, we must sign off, Jo, we're going to fill in our lottery tickets and then go back to reopen the salon. Thousands and thousands of kisses. The twins who love you.

From: fergus@aardman-studios.uk

To: Jo@tengoldfingers.com

Bonjour beautiful maman. Juste quelques mots to say that Nadine is expecting a bébé only she hasn't dared to tell you yet. We are très très happy. Come bientôt she will need you. Chaud kisses. Fergus.

From: faouz_belle@faouz_belle.be
To: Jo@tengoldfingers.com

Hello Madame Guerbette.

My name is Faouzia, I live in Knokke-le-Zoute where I met your husband. He was always talking about you and your haberdashery shop and your website; he sometimes cried and he paid me to comfort him. I was only doing my job and I'm sure you won't think too badly of me. Before he left he gave me a Patek watch and I only recently found out what it's really worth so I thought it ought to go back to you. Please tell me where I can send it. I am so sorry about what happened to you. Faouzia.

From: maelysse.quemener@gmail.fr

To: Jo@tengoldfingers.com

I am looking for some seagull-grey stranded embroidery thread, do you have any? And do you know whether there are any crochet workshops in the Bénedoit area? I'd be glad to find out. Thank you for your help.

Acknowledgements

My thanks to the amazing Karina Hocine.

To Emmanuelle Allibert, the most delightful of press attachées.

To Claire Silve and her invigorating demands.

To Grâce, Sibylle and Raphaële, who were Jocelyne's first three friends.

To all the bloggers and readers who have been encouraging me since I wrote *L'Écrivain de la Famille*, and whose enthusiasm and friendship prompted the joy with which I wrote this one.

To all the bookshops who backed my first novel.

To Valérie Brotons-Bedouk, who introduced me to *The Marriage of Figaro*.

And finally to Dana, who is the ink behind it all.

Reading Group Notes

A Note from Grégoire Delacourt on *The List of My Desires*

Have you ever noticed that when you choose something, you often ask yourself if it wouldn't have been better to choose something else? We quickly grow tired of the things we possess. We make the longevity of things – the fact that they last – the source of our unhappiness. Oh, if only I had a new telephone! If only my wife were blonde! If only I could own that red car! I would be so much happier if . . .

And so, with *The List of My Desires*, there came the idea of a life that could be rewritten, reinvented; a life in which one could rub out the grey and replace it with green, or blue. A life in which one could appreciate what one already possessed – and savour it.

That is how the idea for this book was born.

I was going to give a character, someone deep in middle age, the chance to change their life.

And, like a magic wand, there appeared the idea of an impressive win on the lottery (I could equally have made a genie appear from a lamp, but that idea had already been used and was rather well done!).

And so, since this was about the list of my desires, there also came this idea – to be a woman for the duration of the book. I wanted to write this story through the words of a woman, the way she saw things, her kindness, her wisdom (even if I know full well that women aren't always wise!).

And that is how I became Jocelyne, the owner of a haberdashery in a little town in the north of France; a woman who had a life like everyone else, with its highs and lows, and who suddenly had the possibility to erase everything she didn't like about her life.

But of course it is just when we are on the point of losing something that we suddenly understand its true value . . .

For Discussion

1. What would you have done in Jocelyne's shoes? If you had cashed the cheque, what would you have spent the money on?

2. *I'd like to have the chance to decide what my life will be like. I think that's the best present anyone can get.*
   Why is Jocelyne's life so different from the future she imagined when she was seventeen?

3. *Women are the fingers and the hand is their passion.*
   Why does Jocelyne's blog appeal to so many women?

4. Why is Jocelyne unconvinced that money

can make her happy? Were you willing her to cash the cheque as you read or did you empathise with her hesitations?

5. *You're a wonderful husband, Jo, I think; a big brother, a father, you're all the men a woman can need.*
   And maybe even an enemy too.
   How would you describe Jocelyne's relationship with her husband, Jo?

6. Why is Jo unfulfilled by his new life as a millionaire?

7. Should Jocelyne have stayed with Jo when his behaviour changed after the death of Nadège? Can you understand why she stayed?

8. Jocelyne makes four lists. One is a list of things she needs, the second is a wish list, the third is a list of crazy notions and then she makes her final list. How do these lists change as the book progresses?

9. *Grief refashions you in a strange form.*
    How does Jo's betrayal change Jocelyne?

10. Does *The List of My Desires* have a happy ending? Is Jocelyne's new life better than the life she had before?

11. Did reading *The List of My Desires* change your views on whether money or material objects can make you happy?

12. Jocelyne is an everywoman but her creator, Grégoire Delacourt, is a man. Did knowing that change the way you read *The List of My Desires*? Does it matter?

Suggested Further Reading

The Elegance of the Hedgehog by Muriel Barbery

No and Me by Delphine de Vigan

The President's Hat by Antoine Laurain

The Particular Sadness of Lemon Cake
by Aimee Bender

Chocolat by Joanne Harris

The Unlikely Pilgrimage of Harold Fry
by Rachel Joyce

The Puppet Boy of Warsaw by Eva Weaver

Ten Lottery Facts

- The largest prize ever won in Europe was €180 million (£161 million), won by a Scottish EuroMillions ticket holder on 12th July 2011.
- The first lotteries are thought to have taken place during the Chinese Han Dynasty, between 205 and 177 BC, and were used to help finance The Great Wall of China.
- The Dutch *Staatsloterij* is the oldest running national lottery.
- Over 20 million viewers tuned in to watch the first UK National Lottery show on BBC 1.
- The first French lottery, the *Loterie Royale*, was held in 1539.
- France is Europe's luckiest country as far as EuroMillions jackpot winners are concerned. The nation has had more top prize winners

than any other participating country.

- The odds of winning any prize in the EuroMillions are 1 in 13. The chances of winning the jackpot are 1 in 116,531,800 and the chances of winning the UK national lottery jackpot are 1 in 13,983,816.
- In the time of the Roman Empire, lotteries were a popular amusement at dinner parties.
- When the UK National Lottery first began in 1994 there were five machines from which the balls were drawn, named Arthur, Galahad, Guinevere, Lancelot and Merlin.
- The luckiest EuroMillions number is 50; it has been drawn 39 times since the game launched.
- The longest lottery celebration ever was by a pub syndicate in London and lasted two weeks.

**If you enjoyed *The List of My Desires*,
then you'll love Grégoire's next novel,**

The First Thing You See

What you see isn't always what you get ...

Arthur Dreyfuss, an unassuming young mechanic, leads a simple life in a sleepy French village. Then, one night, he opens his door to find a distraught Hollywood actress standing before him.

But this woman is not all she seems. For her real name is Jeanine Foucamprez, and her story is very different from the glamorous life of the star she resembles. Arthur is not all he seems, either; a reader of poetry with a tragic past, he dreams of being the kind of hero that leading ladies fall in love with.

Is this the meeting of kindred souls? Can Arthur look beyond the surface and see Jeanine for who she really is?

Turn over for an extract from the novel ...

Scarlett Johansson looked exhausted.

Her hair, somewhere in between two colours, was at war with itself, tumbling loose, flowing, as if in slow motion. Her luscious mouth had lost its usual gloss. There were gloomy shadows beneath her eyes where her mascara had smudged, like charcoal. And unfortunately for Arthur Dreyfuss, she was wearing a baggy sweater. A sweater like a sack that did no justice to the actress's curves, which everyone knew were bewitching, spellbinding.

She was holding a Vuitton bag in acid colours that made it look like a fake.

As for Arthur Dreyfuss, he was wearing what he usually wore to watch TV: a white undershirt and a pair of boxer shorts sporting a picture of the Smurfs. A long way from the image of Ryan-Gosling-only-better-looking.

All the same, as soon as they set eyes on each other they smiled.

Did they find one another handsome? Or reassuring? Perhaps, when there was such an urgent knocking on his door, Arthur had expected trouble with a cylinder head gasket, or a big end going, problems with a flow meter? When he opened the door, had she been expecting a pervert, a witch covered with warts, an old lady with a sweet little face? Whatever the case, it is a fact that the unlikely couple smiled as if pleasantly surprised, and Arthur Dreyfuss, who had just fallen in love at first sight for the second time in his life and was suffering the side effects (sweaty hands, rapid heartbeat, beads of perspiration, glacial little scalpels digging into his back, a frozen tongue) opened his dry mouth and uttered a word that does not exist.

Comine.

(For enquiring readers who take an interest in linguistics, and for amateur geographers, we may as well point out that there is, in fact, a town called Comines in the canton of Quesnoy-sur-Deûle in northern France, near the Belgian border – probably a rather sleepy little place, since there are at least five committees in the town trying to organise festivals to shake it up – but that has nothing to do with the present story.)

The moment Arthur Dreyfuss saw Scarlett Johansson standing in his doorway, his timid *Comine* instinctively struck him as the most appropriate, most courteous, and in general the best thing to say, because, according to the subtitles for the TV series that he was watching in the original version, those words were the English equivalent of '*Entrez*'.

And what man in the world, even one wearing an undershirt and boxer shorts with Smurfs on them, would not have said '*Comine*' to the amazing star of *Lost in Translation*?

The amazing star whispered, '*Thank you*', in English, the pink tip of her tongue showing between her lips as she pronounced the *th*, and came in.

As he quietly closed the door, hands sweating and heart suddenly switching up into an even higher gear – yes, he was going to die, and yes, he *could* die happy now – Arthur glanced furtively round to see if there were cameras outside, and/or bodyguards, and/or some professional practical joker from a TV station. Then, still not entirely reassured, he bolted the door.

Two years earlier, the police had brought a car into PP's garage, the wreck of a Peugeot 406 that had just somersaulted five times on the D112 near Cocquerel (2.42 kilometres away from Long as the crow flies).

It was night.

The driver had been going fast; he seemed to have lost control of the car, skidding on the treacherous layer of water that oozed like translucent algae from the uneven surface of the country road where it passed the Étangs des

Provisions. The two occupants had died instantly. The firemen had had to cut off the man's legs to get him out of the car. The passenger's face had been crushed against the windscreen and a lock of her blonde hair was caught in the star-shaped patch of glass, together with a lozenge of blood. When, on PP's instructions, he had examined the interior of the wreck, Arthur Dreyfuss had found a book of poetry on the passenger seat and instantly, as if by a reflex action, tucked it into one of the large pockets of his dungarees. What was a poetry book doing in a car where two people had just died? Had the passenger been reading the driver a poem when the car came off the road? Who were they? Were they leaving each other, or meeting each other again? Had they decided to put an end to it all together?

That evening, alone in his little house, Arthur had opened the book, his fingers trembling slightly. The collection was entitled *Existing*, and the author's name was Jean Follain. There was a lot of white on each page, and in the middle of it short lines, little furrows carved out by the ploughshare of letters. He read simple words that seemed to describe very profound things, like these, which evoked for him his father:

> . . . and beneath his strong arm
> Not even looking at the trees
> he doggedly held
> all the figures of the world.[*]

And these, which might have been about Noiya and their mother:

> . . . and here is she who will die young
> and she whose body alone is left.[†]

There wasn't a word that he failed to understand, but the way they were put together astonished him. He had a confused feeling that words he knew, if ornamented with pearls in a certain way, could change his perception of the world.

[*] Jean Follain, 'Atlas', *Territoires* (Gallimard, 1953).
[†] Jean Follain, 'Les Enfants', *Territoires* (Gallimard, 1953).

Could celebrate the grace of ordinary things, for instance – ennobling the simple.

Over the next few months he relished the other wonderful arrangements of words in the book. To him, they seemed like a gift that might help tame the extraordinary, if ever it should come knocking at the door.

For instance on Wednesday, 15 September 2010, at 7.47 in the evening, when the stunning Scarlett Johansson, American actress born on 22 November 1984 in New York, was suddenly standing in front of you, Arthur Dreyfuss, French motor mechanic, an astounded Longinian, born in 1990.

How could it be possible?

And introducing ...

We Only Saw Happiness

Grégoire Delacourt's Prix Goncourt-longlisted novel.

Available now from W&N

Antoine's parents fell in love at first sight. But they quickly realised that true love means more than furtive glances. Married too young, and with three small children, Antoine's mother retreats into a world of Sagan novels and cigarette smoke, abandoning the family when Antoine's sister dies. He grows up with a distant father, his only respite the tenderness he shares with his surviving sister.

Then Antoine meets Natalie, the woman of his dreams. They have two children and Antoine thrives in his work for an insurance company, investigating claims to reduce his firm's pay-outs. But soon Natalie drifts away from him, beginning an affair, and Antoine loses his job when he lets his heart overrule his head. Driven to despair, he does something unspeakable. Antoine's journey to come to terms with the terrible thing he has done will take him across seas and continents, deep into his own heart and the hearts of others, as he is forced to question what a life is really worth.